Old Morals, Small Continents, Darker Times

The Iowa School of Letters Award for Short Fiction

PHILIP F. O'CONNOR

Old Morals,
Small Continents,
Darker Times

University of Iowa Press **Ψ** Iowa City

The previously published stories in this collection appear by permission:

"The Gift Bearer," *Southern Review* (1970)
"Story Hour," *four quarters* (1970)
"Matter of Ages," *The Smith* (1968)
"American Gothic," *December* (1968)
"Funeral," *Colorado State Review* (1968)
"A San Francisco Woman," *Forum* (1970)
"Donovan, the Cat Man," *Transatlantic Review* (1967)
"The Thumping of the Grass," *Quartet* (1970)
"Powers Being Himself," *Wisconsin Review* (1969)
"Gerald's Song," *Western Humanities Review* (1969)
"Mastodon's Box," *Transatlantic Review* (1971)

Title changes and revisions have been made on several stories.

"The Gift Bearer" is included in *Best American Short Stories of 1971,* edited by Martha Foley and David Burnett (Boston, 1971).

The author is grateful for a writing grant awarded to him during the summer of 1967 by Clarkson College of Technology, Potsdam, N. Y.

Library of Congress Catalog Card Number: 70-158043
University of Iowa Press, Iowa City 52240
© 1971 by Philip F. O'Connor. All rights reserved
Printed in the United States of America
ISBN 87745-023-4

For Delores
 Dondi
 John
 Christopher
 Erin
 and
 Justin
And in memory of my parents
 John and Josephine

Contents

Foreword

When we first announced our annual award
for a volume of short fiction, we were confident that there
were a number of writers with collections of stories they
might be interested in contributing. The confidence was
not misplaced. This year, only the second, we received
exactly 250 entries. To be sure, not all of the manuscripts were impressive. A good many contained only
two or three excellent stories; few sustained a high level
of artistry throughout. But the total accomplishment
represented by all of the entries indicated that writers
continue to find the short story a useful form for the
shaping of their observations and ideas.

Each of the 250 manuscripts was carefully read by
William Murray or by one or more of his aides in the
Iowa Writers Workshop. The twenty that they deemed
outstanding were then read by the entire fiction staff of
the Workshop, and the six *they* thought the best were
sent to George Elliott, director of the writing program
at Syracuse University. Mr. Elliott selected this volume
by Philip O'Connor as the best of them all. The decision
can hardly be considered a surprise. Although this is
Mr. O'Connor's first book-length collection, some thirty
stories of his have appeared singly in the little magazines
—which are now about the only outlet for quality short
fiction.

As Mr. Murray has pointed out, the present volume should be read as a progression. The early stories, although not rigorously sociological, suggest Mr. O'Connor's own Irish-American boyhood. The locale is San Francisco, but it might well be Boston or New York. As the collection proceeds, the stories move out of the milieu of innocence and childhood and into the adult world of experience. Characters confront hopelessness, despair, and insanity, and try to arrive at some measure of security through the purgatory of experience. O'Connor himself says that he likes to find characters in desperate situations where there is only a flicker of hope that they may come out on top.

Particularly noticeable is the change in these stories from the realistic mode of the opening pieces to a terse kind of lyricism evidenced in such works as "The Thumping of the Grass," "Gerald's Song," and "Mastodon's Box." This lyrical experimentation in the last five stories, it seems clear, could not have come off so well had Mr. O'Connor not subjected himself to the discipline of the more conservative earlier ones. Though he moves away from naturalism he retains his respect for the sharply observed detail, the exact phrase, the character whom we come to understand in large part as a product of his environment. Mr. O'Connor's accomplishment in short is very considerable, one well worth the Iowa School of Letters Award.

John Gerber, Director
School of Letters
The University of Iowa

Philip F. O'Connor

Philip F. O'Connor has been writing and publishing stories for eight years. A native San Franciscan, he holds graduate degrees from San Francisco State College and The University of Iowa. Recently he resigned as director of the graduate writing program at Bowling Green State University in order to give more of his time to writing.

The Gift Bearer

Uncle Dave had a great knot of a nose, scarlet and bumpy, and he visited us about twice a year. On his last visit, the one I remember best, he brought, as was his habit, a gift for each of us: for my mother "a little thing for the house," a flat package wrapped in brown paper and twine which she sniffed at and hummed over (unappreciatively, I thought) and then put on the top shelf of the kitchen cupboard; for my father a heavy carton which he and my uncle removed carefully from the trunk of his Model A, carried to the basement and placed delicately under the little work bench; and for me a stack of comic books, mostly *Walt Disney's*, which were all wrinkled like the magazines and comic books at the town's barber shop.

After handing my mother and me our gifts, he rubbed his hands briskly together, looked from one of us to the other, said loudly, "I hope ·all present are happy and well," then sat down to supper, the meal for which he had arrived, as usual, just in time. Before we finished eating he reached across the table and scratched the top of my head with his rough fingers. "It's a short life, Jackie," he said, "and time we made the best of it."

The remark, which he always made sooner or later after entering the house, was like a signal for my mother to start the dishes and my father to say, "Shall we take a little spin around the neighborhood, Dave?" It was magic in a way, for it never failed to set my parents kind of invisibly apart, where they remained until his visit ended.

"Make the best of it," my mother repeated mockingly to my father after the two men had returned from their spin and Dave had gone to bed. "He's the last man on earth to be talking about making the best of anything."

My father, on a wooden chair in the narrow space between a cupboard and the kitchen window, only grunted uneasily and said, "Give the man a chance, will you? Give him a bit of a chance."

"A chance," she said derisively from the sink, where she picked up a wet dish cloth and began, fiercely, to wring it dry. "Isn't that a laugh? He's frittered away most of his sixty-two years doing you-know-what and now you talk about giving him a chance." She looked at me over her shoulder and clicked her tongue disgustedly. "Did you hear that, Jackie? Give the man a chance?"

I wasn't about to take sides. Taking sides might have meant a commitment for the duration of my uncle's stay, offering moral and other kinds of support to the parent with whom I allied myself, cutting myself off from the other. At nine years I still felt too unsteady to stand without the security of both pillars. I only nodded politely.

My father was gazing at the fading red design on the linoleum, his shoulders down, looking smaller and thinner than he really was. "I don't know," he said weakly. "If you ask me it's an awfully poor way to talk about your own flesh and blood."

She pulled the string on the small light above the sink and turned around, crossing her arms beneath her large breasts. "Where did you two go after supper?" she said coldly. The only light now in the kitchen shone from the hall, fell full on her, making her, a big woman to begin with, seem whitely enormous.

2

"We just drove out to the edge of town to get a look at those new houses that're going up."

"Did you?"

"We did."

"And that's all?"

"Ah well. Nearly all." My father, who had been reduced to a shadow in the diminished light, twisted uncomfortably.

"You stopped at Henry's, I'll wager."

"For a drop is all."

"By the watery eyes of you it was more than a drop."

No sound issued from the corner.

"I will not have a repeat of what happened at the train station last year." She spoke severely. "Not that or anything approaching it."

"How," said my father in tremulous voice, "did you learn about that?"

"It isn't any of your business but if you must know it was one of the ladies in the sodality. She was waiting for the four-twenty to San Francisco and witnessed the whole thing. I nearly fell down dead when she told me. Imagine! Singing in public with your arms up!" She gave me a guilty look, seeming to realize she'd said a little more than she wanted me to hear.

"It, it wasn't as bad as she made out."

"Hah! And how do you know, not having heard her?"

"I, I can imagine."

"I'm sure it takes little imagining."

"Well, it was only once. I never did anything like it before or since."

"Nor ever will again if I have anything to say about it." She turned to him, scowling. "If I get a whiff of that poison in the next few days, he's going out of here, bag and baggage." My father started to reply, but she cut him off—"Him, or me and Jackie!"—and rumbled off to bed.

My father shook his head as though it weighed a ton,

3

Philip F. O'Connor

pulled himself up and started slowly for the door. He let out a sigh and mumbled, "A fella'd have to be made of steel to put up with the likes of her." He shuffled into the hall, looking more like rubber than steel.

The next morning I was sitting on the edge of the bathtub watching, fascinated, as my uncle shaved with his thick-handled brush, straight razor, and black mug, which had D. O'G. (for David O'Gorman) in fancy gold letters painted on the front and contained soap that smelled like a mountain. I heard the door open and turned to see my father bend low, raise his hand to his mouth and whisper cautiously, "Mag's on the warpath. Don't touch a drop 'til I get home. Not a drop."

Dave, with brush poised at the tip of his chin, had raised his head like a person who's just heard a suspicious sound in his basement. He stood very still until after my father, giving him an apologetic look, had shut the door. Then he reached up slowly and with thumb and forefinger squeezed the remaining soap out of his brush, sending it—splat!—perfectly into the hole at the bottom of the sink. His sole comment.

I knew war was unavoidable. I knew it as well as I knew what was in the carton in the basement or why my father's eyes were glassy or why the neighborhood only interested him when Dave was present. I knew it because I knew the reason for my mother's ultimatum the night before. I had witnessed the incident at the train station. I had, in fact, borne the memory of it like a hidden sore for nearly a year.

I was returning along the railroad tracks from the town's baseball diamond one Saturday afternoon when I heard a voice up ahead of me, a voice I recognized, calling out, "C'mon now, every one of you join in with us. Sure, you only live once!" I looked up, stunned, to see Uncle Dave and my father standing on the station platform. It was Dave who had spoken, and now my

4

father raised his hands and started waving them like a spastic orchestra leader. Before I could move or even think, the two of them started singing, in grating counterpoint, the first few verses of "Sweet Rose of Dublin." No one joined them. In fact, the onlookers seemed disgusted, except for one or two men, who were smiling. By the time I had run, humiliated, behind a tree not far from the tracks, the two had stopped their attempts to form a choral group and were on their way across the street to the place called Henry's, which, until then, I had thought was only a restaurant.

It was the first time I'd seen either Dave or my father behaving peculiarly, and it so horrified me that I got sick on the way home and threw up behind a neighbor's hedge. I went to bed soon after that and I wept into the night, into many nights in fact. I never said anything to my mother, for I was afraid her reaction would be as fierce as mine, or worse. I was relieved now to learn that she'd found out what had happened, though I knew it must have been terrible for her.

Dave and I sat on the front porch swing late that afternoon, waiting for my father to come down the street from work. The brisk western breeze, cutting between mountains that separated our little valley from the Pacific, made the wisteria branches rattle against eaves and crept across the porch, cooling us after a very warm day. It was a nice afternoon for a conversation.

"Uncle Dave," I said, after we'd been going squeakily forward and back for several minutes, "is it all right if I ask you a question?"

He put the palm of his thick hand on my knee and said, very seriously, "Do you know what uncles were made for?"

I told him I didn't.

"Hah," he said, making the swing stop, "I thought you didn't. Well, I'll tell you." He inhaled noisily and let the air out by opening and closing his mouth with little pop-ping sounds. "Uncles," he said, "were made to answer questions." He looked down at me, smiling. "You didn't know that, eh?"

"No," I said, shaking my head. "Nobody ever told me."

He made a clicking sound with his tongue. "I wonder what sort of things they teach in school these days, if it isn't what uncles are for?"

I started reeling off some of my school subjects, but he wasn't listening.

"It's a shame," he said, "an unforgivable shame." He inhaled once more and once more popped the air out. "I've always thought it a crime you weren't born and raised in the old country. Everything is different, *ev*-verything. The weather, the schools, the people. *Ev*-verything."

I believed him. Listening to him and my father and even my mother when they spoke about Ireland, I longed to visit there. From what I'd gathered there were a lot of hills, and the children spent more time in the hills than in schools or churches, and they weren't always (as I increasingly was) told to excel in this or that; they just sort of made their own way at their own pace and spent the evenings around the kitchen fire listening to their parents and their relatives and the neighbors tell stories about saints appearing and about banshees and leprechauns, the kind of stories I only heard when Dave came to our house.

He sat quietly for a few minutes, then said, "Did I ever tell you the time we were caught in the rowboat out in the Irish Channel during a storm, my two friends and I?

"Yes." (One of the friends clung to the overturned boat while Dave and the other swam two, four or six miles—depending on the telling—for help. Unfortunately, about half-way to land the other swimmer collapsed and Dave had to pull him along. As, himself weakened by the extra weight, Dave was about to go under with his load, he spotted a fishing boat in the distance. It was quite far away, and the storm was making an awful howl. Still he called, louder than he could have imagined the human voice being able to cry out. "The sound," he said, "seemed to flatten the swells." Again and again he called. Finally the little boat turned toward them. Eventually all three of them were picked up and saved. "You'll notice," he always said when he came to the end of the story, "that I have a very deep voice." I nodded, for it was true, deep and penetrating with a crack of finality to it. "Well, I got that by calling out to the fishing boat.") "You told me this story," I said, "but I would like to hear it again." I looked at his broad hands and hard round forearms and wondered if those, too, had resulted from his adventures at sea.

He told me the story again, but he hurried through it, leaving out several parts. When he finished, he glanced through the vines toward the corner of the street. "What time does your daddy usually get home?" he said with a touch of impatience.

"Quarter-to-six," I said.

He frowned. "I thought it was five-thirty."

"No." I was certain. "Quarter-to-six."

He started to push the swing forward and back. As he did so he slipped his hand into a front pants' pocket and removed a large round watch, one I always liked seeing and holding because it had very black numbers on the face and ticked very loudly, so loudly you could hear it when it was in his pocket. "It's only fifteen apast five," he said disgustedly.

"Maybe you have time to tell me a story then."

Pop pop. His mouth was at it. He wasn't listening to me. Pop pop. He took out his watch again, just to make sure.

"Uncle Dave?"

"Eh?"

7

Philip F. O'Connor

"Do you have time for a story?"

The swing stiffened against my back. Uncle Dave let out a long dreary sigh. At last he said, "All right, all right," and he told a story. He told it with a terrible rapidity but with a terrible intensity too. From the way he spoke I doubt if he left out even a phrase:

There was a farming man from the town of Ballyanne who had only one pleasure in his life, and that pleasure was spending a single evening out of every week at a well-known gathering place, one where the conversation was always marked with good cheer and happiness. The woman he lived with, however (she was said by some to be his wife, though the man himself was never known to admit it), took a foul view of his one simple joy and sought to put a stop to it. She claimed to the parish priest and others bent on taking her side that the man was spending all their money and returning home in a hard and vicious mood to rebuke her at every opportunity. He denied the charges, of course, pointing out that the woman ("Look at the size of her," he said.) clearly ate well on the money he made. He added that all the little visits did was loosen the muscles in his tongue which had gone tight after six days of living with her do's and don'ts. It was quite an argument and there was little question in the minds of most of the townspeople as to who was right and who was wrong. After hearing both sides the great majority of them spoke the cause of the man, many of them saying they'd never known him to open his mouth except in laughter and song. This blackguardly woman, however, was not to be stopped. She devised a scheme which she thought would once and for all put an end to his happy excursions. Recalling that he had a terrible fear of ghosts, she planned a little surprise for him and fixed the location for it in a small cemetery he had to pass on his way to and from the village. As he was coming home late one night he saw, rising up from one of the graves that had just been dug

8

near the road, a ghastly figure as if from another world. It was dressed all in white and crying out in terrible anguish. "I am so cold and lonely," said the headless creature in a mysterious voice. It was, of course, none other than the woman herself. In trying to scare him forever from his weekly pleasure, however, she had neglected to take into account one small but not widely known fact: among other things that his weekly trips loosened in the man was his fear of the unknown. As with speech and his woman, so did they liberate him from the terror of ghosts. It was, indeed, a bad miscalculation on the woman's part, for the man only looked calmly at the strange figure and said, "It's no wonder you're cold and lonely. You haven't been properly buried." With that he rushed over and picked up the gravedigger's shovel and furiously began to fill in the deep grave. As the dirt came down upon her the woman shouted, "Stop, Jerry! It's me! It's only me!" but the man kept shovelling. As the dirt began to cover up her legs she cried out, "Don't you hear me at all? Don't you hear me!" The man, giving no sign of hearing anything, moved like a fiend and did not stop until the noisy creature was all covered up. Some say it was because of the drink that he didn't hear and others say his ears had long since gone deaf to the sound of the woman's voice. No one knows for sure. What is known is that she was neither seen nor heard from since. And the man thereafter spent many a happy night in the village with his companions.

It was a wonderful story, and I was about to tell him so when he stirred, reaching into his pocket, pulling out his watch, looking. "Good," he said, "good. Twenty minutes to." He glanced down at me. "Where's your mother now?"

"In the back yard, I think, taking down some wash." I had heard the screen door bang closed and then the clothesline begin squeaking.

"Ah, fine," he said. "Now you go in the kitchen and open the ice box." He flicked his fingers, signalling me to get up. "Take the chunk of ice I knocked off the big block after lunch today and carry it down to the basement. Put it in the pan I left on your father's tool bench." He pointed to the front door. "Hurry now, hurry!"

I did just what he said.

When I got back to the porch, he was looking up the street, where my father had just turned the corner and was walking toward us.

"God, it's a wonderful cool afternoon, isn't it?" Dave said, noticing me at his side.

The question, his happy tone, caught me by surprise.

"You did what I asked you to, didn't you?" he went on.

I told him I had.

He put his hand on the back of my neck as we stood watching my father, who seemed to be picking up speed. He said, "I seem to remember that our little conversation of a few minutes ago began with you about to ask me a question." He took his eyes from my father long enough to look down at me. "What was it?"

I thought for a few moments, recalled it had something to do with them singing at the train station last year but couldn't remember the details. "I don't know," I said.

"It must be a question that oughtn't be asked." He sounded like a bishop making an important pronouncement.

"Hey, John," he called as my father neared the front yard. "Go in the basement quiet as a mouse and we'll have a quick one before you take off your hat. It's been an awful long day."

My father looked down the driveway to the back yard, I guess to make sure my mother hadn't heard Dave's instructions, and then, taking no chances calling back, raised his hand with thumb and forefinger forming a circle, flicked it at Dave, and rushed toward the basement door.

"Atta boy," said Uncle Dave breathlessly, and he turned and hurried across the porch and down the front stairs.

They didn't make it upstairs to supper. My mother took their absence with surprising calm. As we waited in the kitchen, listening to them get louder and louder just below us, she only tapped the big wooden spoon she had been using to prepare the meal against the edge of the sink and made occasional hissing sounds. Finally she looked at me and said, "Where did he catch him, on the way down the street?"

I nodded, knowing how disappointed she must have felt at not intercepting my father before my uncle had. When she got to him first, there was a good chance he'd keep himself from the basement or the jaunt through "the neighborhood." Around Dave he seemed to have no will, or maybe it was only a different sort of will.

"I thought it wouldn't happen 'til tomorrow," she said, as much to herself as to me. "He usually holds off for a couple of days trying to get on the good side of me." She was, of course, speaking of Dave. She sounded as though she wasn't going to let their vanishing act disturb her at all.

She remained calm for only a short time, however. When supper was ready, she smacked the head of the spoon loudly against the sink and sputtered, "There'll be retribution for this. There'll be retribution." She turned off the burner under the pot of stew that had been simmering all day. "Sit down," she said to me, "and eat your supper."

Later that evening, on the pretext of going to the baseball diamond near our home to watch the older boys play ball, I circled to the back yard determined to get my first look at the clandestine undertaking that was causing so much trouble.

I crept along the wall at the back of the house until I came to a small window looking in on the brightly lit corner where they sat.

My father was on the stool before his work bench. (He had only a few tools—a hammer, a screwdriver, a hacksaw, and a pair of pliers—all nailed awkwardly to the wall behind the bench.) He gripped, on the work bench, a large green bottle, which was, it seemed to me, about two-thirds full. In the hand which rested on his lap was a small glass from which, as he spoke to Dave, there dropped—plunk plunk—little splashes of whiskey.

Dave himself was a few feet away in a kitchen chair on the concrete floor, looking up at my father. Dave's glass was nearly full, but he held it straight without even looking at it and not a drop was spilling. Between his feet was the pan of ice I had taken from the kitchen, only now the ice was smaller and floating in its own water. I put my ear very close to the window so as to hear what my father, whose mouth was moving with unusual speed, was saying.

"If she were to open that door right now, do you know what I'd tell her, Dave?"

Uncle Dave gave an inquisitive grunt.

"I'd say, 'There are certain portions of a home that are to be the man's alone. And certain times of the day when he is to be left to do what he wants. And certain companions he's to enjoy by himself. I'd also say, 'There's no one! Not you! Not the Pope! Not Jesus himself! No one who can ever change that!' I'd say, 'These are as much a part of being a man as, as the hair on his face!'" He raised his glass to his lips, took a sip and gave a confident little nod. "That's what I'd say."

"God," said Dave, shaking his white-capped head in unrestrained appreciation, "If I thought you had it in you, I'd be greatly encouraged. Greatly."

12

"Well, I do. As sure as your sitting there. As sure as that." He raised his forefinger generally toward the top of the basement stairs. "All she has to do is open that door."

I was troubled at hearing my father speak of my mother as though she were bent on taking from him all the things he cared about. It bothered me, too, that he had certain times and places and friends (not including me) he wanted only for himself. (I'd suspected as much but only now had had it confirmed.) It shocked me to see his eyes dancing about madly, and his hands moving strangely, and his voice with a roughness in it I'd never known. But more than all this, I was desperately curious. I peered through the window, as though, looking harder, I would find the key to the horrible scene I was witnessing.

Dave was speaking. "They say the curse of the Irish is whiskey." The mention of the word "whiskey" seemed to remind him of what was in his glass, for he paused, looked down and then, in one unbelievable gulp, swallowed the entire contents. "Boowahhh! . . . But it's not whiskey at all. Do you know what it really is?"

"I think I do."

"It's woman, that's what it is."

"Dead right on the money. Here." My father brought the bottle forward and refilled Dave's upraised glass. "From the womb to the tomb," he said. He then filled his own.

I noticed for the first time that my father still had his hat on. It was tilted back on his balding head like the hat of a college boy I'd seen in an advertisement for a movie about the twenties. Everything I now observed set him farther apart from me. It struck me that if I knelt at that window long enough he would, Jekyll and Hyde, soon become completely unrecognizable. College boy indeed! How ridiculous he began to seem. I wanted to crash through the window and put a stop to everything.

They sat quietly for quite a while before my father

13

spoke again, this time with a new weariness. "But it's life and we have to accept it. If you know that, you're ahead of the game. Am I right or wrong?"

My uncle shrugged and took another long swallow.

"Ah, it's the truth, Dave, and we're all better with knowing it."

Dave did not reply. He seemed to be getting very uncomfortable, fidgeting, looking nervously about the basement, which was completely dark except for the small space around the work bench, fixing his eyes finally on the carton beneath the bench.

I saw now, as I looked at it along with Dave, that the cardboard flaps were pulled all the way back and that it was full of bottles. Rather, nearly full, for one bottle, the one they were drinking from, was missing. Whiskey, as my mother had often reminded my father, was terribly expensive. Looking at that carton I thought Dave must be very rich. I really didn't know, however.

What I knew about Dave was that he had run away from his home in Ireland as a youth, had worked with his hands all his life, and had never married. He now lived alone in Bakersfield (or was it Santa Barbara?), sold used furniture (or was it cars?), came to visit us once or twice a year, brought gifts and got in trouble with my mother for leading my father astray. My own great uncle but still a very mysterious man.

"I can't agree at all," Dave said at last. "You go around accepting all the malarky they give you, and you aren't but a shred of a man anymore." He knocked off his last glassful—"Booowahhh!"—and looked steadily at my father.

"Ah well," said my father even more wearily, "maybe you're right, maybe you're right. I've never had it completely figured out."

My uncle smiled and said, "I don't think either one of us is going to solve the problems of the world sitting

14

here. Let's go down and see how business is holding up at Hen-e-ry's."

"Now there's something," said my father, straightening his hat, "over which there can be no debate."

They went out the side door laughing.

I walked slowly upstairs and found my mother in the living room. She was listening to a program of Irish music from San Francisco and sewing a patch on the elbow of one of my flannel shirts. "They're gone for the night," she said. "I just heard the two of them giggle their way through the door beneath me. Did you happen to pass them on the street?"

I said no and then kissed her goodnight, more tenderly than I had kissed her in months.

I had no idea when they returned from Henry's, but knew it must have been very late, for Uncle Dave didn't get up until nearly noon, and my father remained in his bedroom even later than that. Luckily it was Saturday, and my father did not have to go to work.

My first look at Dave convinced me that, for all the apparent joy in drinking, its aftermath was Hell itself. I found him in the kitchen when I came in for lunch. A trembling apparition, he was standing in the doorway, his nose virtually aflame, his eyes buried deep in his swelled-up face. He was looking at my mother, who was on a little stool at the sink peeling turnips, and ignoring him. As I closed the screen door and headed for the sandwich my mother had set out for me on the table, he clapped his hands together and his mouth cracked open in a brave attempt to smile. "Well," he said, looking from my mother to me, "it seems like another warm one. I don't see a trace of clouds."

I smiled back at him, but my mother didn't look up or speak a word. I saw that at his place at the table, as at my father's, nothing was laid out, not even a spoon or a napkin. A little guiltily I raised half of my sandwich and took a bite. I felt like offering Dave a bite, but it didn't seem the thing to do.

"Yes, sir," he said, taking a cautious step into the kitchen, "a good day for me to do a little work on my car." He took another step. "Just as soon as I get a little fuel—heh—to keep me going."

Now my mother spoke, still not looking up. "I'd've thought you'd put enough fuel in you last night to last the rest of the month. That is, if one is able to judge from the noises you and your friend made coming up the steps at half-past two."

"The light was off, Mag. You left the light off, and we couldn't see the stairs. That's all."

"There was more than the light off," she said, taking a heavy swipe at the turnip in her hand, knocking the top completely off.

"And as far as the time goes," Dave said, "I think you'll find it was closer to twelve than two."

"Two-thirty-three," she said firmly.

"Is that a fact?" he said. "I wouldn't have guessed."

"What is it you want?" she said in an unfriendly voice. "Apple juice?"

"Tomato." He waved his hand. "Don't you get up now. I'll find it."

"I'm not getting up," she said. "It's at the bottom of the ice box."

"Good good." He went quickly to the ice box, found the large can of juice, went to the silverware drawer, fumbled about until he found an opener, shakily fiddled with the top of the can until he got it open, looked frantically about—"It's in the cupboard above the ice box," she said—went to the cupboard, took down the bottle of Worcestershire sauce and shook great beads of it into one of the holes in the can. He then put down the bottle and raised the can to his mouth. As my mother watched in disgust, he poured the contents down his throat in a steady brownish-red stream. The gurgling noise was terrible. When he finished he said, "Gahhhd, Mag,

16

that was a life saver!" put the can on top of the ice box, and guided himself shakily toward the hall.

My mother, still on her little chair beside the sink, still peeling, spoke before he reached the doorway. "When are you leaving, Dave?"

"Huh?"

She repeated her question, pausing between each word. "When. Are. You. Leaving?"

"Well ah . . . I thought I'd stay 'til . . . was planning, that is, to hold on here 'til. . . ." As he spoke he looked at her, and seemed to change his statement as he looked. "Maybe tomorrow . . . or Monday . . . eh?" He was still looking. "Or tonight, for that matter, though I . . . wouldn't want to. . . ."

"That'll be fine," she said, overturning the colander with the turnip peelings in it. "Tonight."

He gave her a disbelieving look. "But . . . but, Mag," he said, "I just got here . . . after nearly a year." He looked at me. "Hardly a chance to visit with the fine growing boy here." He looked pleadingly back at her. "Or you either." He moved toward her. "Give us a few days more."

"Tonight. Or Jackie and I won't stay in the house." She turned on the tap to wash her peeled turnips. "And that's as final as anything I've ever said."

Though I hadn't expected my mother to be friendly, I was surprised at her iciness, as surprised as I was at Dave's timidity. How strange my world was becoming. Overnight, it seemed, people you thought you knew changed altogether. My father, a mouse in the kitchen, was a lion in the basement. My mother, powerless in the living room, was now in complete command. My uncle, immune to women, was now being stung by one. It was all topsy-turvy, crazy.

It became even crazier when, after lunch, I watched my uncle put a tarpaulin on the dirt driveway, remove his tool kit from the trunk of his car, and then take off

17

several parts of his engine and clean them piece by piece, with a powerful-smelling rag. He had cleaned his engine in our driveway on earlier trips but never so carefully, never when he was in such a shaky condition, and never while talking as much as he did that afternoon.

As I stood behind him watching the pieces of the engine fly onto the tarp, he asked me which of the comic books I liked most of all those he'd brought. I told him I hadn't yet had time to read them. He said that that was too bad, for they were a very rewarding batch. I asked him if he had read them. He said that, indeed, he had. It didn't seem right, a white-haired man reading comic books, and I asked him why.

He came from under the hood then, wiped his hands with a rag, changed the socket on his wrench, looked at me and said, "Because I'm a philosopher."

"You are?"

"I am."

"What," I asked, "is that?"

He went back under the hood. "A philosopher," he said, "is a person who speculates on the world. He tries to make sense of things. I'm not very good at it . . . (He grunted, trying to pull loose a stubborn piece of the engine.) . . . but (grunt grunt) I do my best." He sent his hand back. "Give me that hammer there, will you Jackie?"

I handed him the hammer.

Again he mentioned the comic books. "Now you take Mickey Mouse . . . (bang bang bang) . . . and Donald Duck. The two of them (bang) can . . . (grunt) teach you a lot. For one thing (bang) they're different types. Mickey (bang bang) is a steadier fella than Donald (bang grunt bang). Donald (bang) is . . . (grunt) pretty jumpy, pretty unsteady. The type (grunt) who should never get (bang) married." He came from under the hood without the piece he'd been trying to get, cursed and threw his hammer and wrench onto the tarp.

"Mickey, on the other hand," he said as he wiped his hands, "would make a pretty good husband. He's a kind of dull steady fella. A lad like you might call him 'a good guy.' He'll get his work done, not forget to bring flowers to Minnie, if that's the one he marries, and is a pretty good example for those nephews of his, Morty and Ferdie. But Donald. . . ." He bent down and picked up the wrench and hammer again. "Donald should never get married." He shook his head. "No, sirree. Do you know what I'd do if Donald married that Daisy Duck?"

I told him I didn't.

"I'd stop buying those comic books."

He started to go under the hood once more, but hesitated and looked at me. "Now I'm not saying either of them should or shouldn't get married, but it'd be worse for Donald. Understand?" Once more he started to bend, but paused. "Which of the two do you like, Donald or Mickey? I mean if you had to choose?"

I thought about it and said I guessed I liked Donald, which, for some reason, was true.

He slapped me on the shoulder and said, "Atta boy!"

Then he did go under the hood, pulling and banging for a long time and finally let out a string of curses. He came up without the elusive piece he was after and said, "To hell with it." He cleaned the pieces that were on the tarp, put them back in the engine and then returned his tools to the trunk. It took a long time, and he didn't say much, except to curse when a piece didn't go back easily.

On the way into the house he said, "You know, Jackie, talk is talk. It's only good up to a point." He put his hand on my shoulder and said, "It's the same with philosophy. Only good up to a point. Do you know what I mean?"

I didn't and told him so.

"Someday you will," he said. "Someday, God willing."

My father didn't come out of his room until Uncle Dave had nearly finished packing. He stood reeling as my uncle calmly told him my mother had ordered him to leave. The pupils of my father's eyes had gone to tiny dots like the holes in a soda cracker and, as he listened, they seemed to revolve like toy springs rapidly unwinding. I thought they might jump out of his head and pounce on Dave. When my uncle finished speaking he said, "You're going nowhere. She . . . she hasn't the right."

"Never mind," said Dave. "I know when I'm beaten."

"What about our talk last night? Have you forgotten that?"

"No," he said, "but when they're as determined as she is you don't have a chance."

My father ignored him, chugged to the kitchen, scraping the wall, tripping once, moving as if he wasn't sure he was even headed in the right direction. "What's this all about?" he said after shakily turning the corner at the doorway and coming to a quick halt.

She was at the table, elbows on top of it, looking fierce and immovable. Her eyes set themselves on him like clamps.

My father, looking ridiculous in pajamas which were too large and which he'd buttoned unevenly at the top, advanced a tenuous step. "You've no heart," he said. The statement seemed to have a hundred trap doors, any one of which he could jump out through in a pinch.

She remained a statue.

"Do . . . do you hear me?" he said, pulling up his pajama bottoms, which had begun to slip down.

It wasn't she but Dave's car which sounded in reply. It had started with a couple of backfires in the driveway.

"For God sake," said my father, and, with a panicky look, he grabbed the string of his pajamas, and scrambled through the hall.

In a minute or so, with me right beside him, he was

20

at the window of the Model A. "What the hell are you doing?" he said. "I had her half won over. Stop the engine now and get out of there."

My uncle looked out the car window. "She has us beat." All the spirit I'd felt coming through from him during his talks to me on the porch seemed to have been drained away. He put the car in reverse and with a few clinks and clanks it took him slowly backwards into the street.

The widow lady next door had been pruning some of her roses, and now, with the car out of the way, she could see my father in his pajamas. She made a disgusted noise, dropped her shears and ran up her front stairs, slamming the door behind her.

"The wrinkled witch," my father muttered before calling to Dave, who had turned the car in the street and was about to set off. "Come back here and don't be a fool!"

"Never give up," said Dave enigmatically, waving his hand at us. "You'll see me again. As soon as the climate is better." With a prolonged asthmatic cough the car lurched forward and hippity-hopped toward the corner.

I once more followed my father to the kitchen, where, addressing my mother, who was just as we'd left her, he sounded more definite than he had in days. "I'm camping downstairs until further notice," he said. "No need for you to put my supper on the table either. I'll be eating at Henry's." He turned abruptly and left the kitchen, a lot more steadily than he had a few minutes earlier.

My mother remained right where she was, an open-eyed corpse.

Though my mother a little later returned to her kitchen functions and my father dressed and did a little slow work in the yard, the remainder of the afternoon, for all that passed between them, was as still as a scene in a photograph, and it stayed that way until just before supper time.

I was in my bedroom catching the end of a San Francisco Seals baseball game on the radio, and my father, who had just taken a mattress and some blankets to the basement, was coming up the stairs to change from work clothes to street clothes for his trip to Henry's. We both must have heard her crying at the same time, for we both arrived in the kitchen together.

She was at the table, but not sitting erect as she had been when my father spoke to her earlier. Her head was down, buried in her arms, and she was sobbing like a little girl. Before her lay brown wrapping paper, open, and at the center of it was something framed.

"What's this about? What's this?" My father crossed the kitchen slowly, me at his heels, and stood beside my mother, not, it seems, knowing what else to say. Finally he looked down at what was on the table.

I looked too, saw what was in the frame: something written, inscribed in the round handwriting I'd seen on cards and letters sent us by Uncle Dave from time to time, only the writing here was bigger and blacker and neater than the writing on the cards and letters:

> *There once was a man*
> *   alone like the sea*
> *Who went to visit*
> *   his loved ones three.*
>
> *They gave him food*
> *   and a place to sleep*
> *And sought, as always,*
> *   his love to keep.*
>
> *He prayed in return*
> *   and offered thanks*
> *That they'd held him close*
> *   within their ranks.*

The Gift Bearer

He gave little else,
a few small gifts,
His own way of saying,
"My loneliness lifts."

My mother, gripping the sides of the table, now contained her tears and the girth of her long enough to utter, as if in proclamation, "He's a good man! God knows down deep he's a good man!"

"Ah well," said my father, putting his hand lightly on her shoulder and running his eyes up the wall as if in search of something. "Ah well."

She began to sob.

Finally my father spoke. "Don't forget his drinking. You're right to see the danger in that."

"I know, I know," said my mother, "but I shouldn't have sent him off the way I did."

They went on speaking to each other in low tones, and I retreated to my room.

I lay down on my bed, sadly, expecting to cry. I lay there until the darkness came through the mountains and hammered itself into the town and the house and the room. I didn't cry. I waited but, for some reason, I didn't cry. Finally I closed my eyes and slept.

I remained asleep until my parents, calling me to supper, startled me out of a dream that, on awakening, I found frightful: Dave was alone at the wheel of his little coupe, on a highway that stetched before him like an endless black ribbon. The car was being rocked by a violent wet storm that lifted and spun it and tossed water against and into it with terrible force. His face, up against the windshield, was etched with horror. Suddenly the car began to shrink, quickly, and soon I could no longer see the figure of my uncle, could only hear him crying frantically out to me to help him. But there was nothing I could do.

Strangely, as I lay there reliving the dream, I began to smile, then laugh, mildly at first and then vigorously,

23

joyfully. I did not understand my reaction, but I remember being struck, a little later, with a thought that, though as powerful and relentless as the storm of my dream, seemed to deny the dream's message. It was a complicated thought, but what it came to was this: In some way my uncle could never be changed, harmed or destroyed, never touched. Never. Though the whole world might turn on him there was this part of him that would hold, **go** on, with a bump here and a rattle there, but *would go on,* the same, until his death, maybe even afterwards, the same, the very same as it had been since I'd known him, since even before that, since his birth and even beyond that, perhaps since time first laid hands on earth. What this part of him was, or whether it was good or bad, remained a mystery to me. I knew only that I had heard it in the rumble in his voice, had seen it in the glowing whiteness of his hair, had felt it in the sharp touch of his eyes. I sensed, too, that it had somehow communicated itself to me, was part of me. I might have remained in my room through the night and the next day considering it and the mystery of it had I not remembered what he'd said about being careful not to take words, or was it thoughts, too seriously.

I got up and went to the kitchen, where I joined my parents for a late supper of boiled beef and cabbage with turnips, a favorite of my father. He let me sip the ale he and Dave had brought back from Henry's the night before. My mother said I wouldn't have to help her with the dishes. Throughout the meal they smiled at me often and then began to cluck and coo at each other like a couple of sated pigeons. I fell asleep at the table before I'd even finished my dessert, chocolate pudding my mother had fixed especially for me.

Story Hour

"Sit quietly. Sit quietly and behave your-selves." The nun, the frowning nun who was old, had been telling them about God and wars. "I won't say it again. Sit quietly now."

Martin had no knowledge of wars but God was with him always. God was the holly bush at the back of the priests' house. God was the sweetness of the holly berry if one could taste the holly berry. Martin was looking now at the holly bush at the back of the priests' house, between the priests' house and the priests' garage. How gleaming were its leaves, and the berries bristled red like drops of blood.

"And Jesus said, 'You shall be soldiers unto My Father.'"

Martin was seven-and-a-half, nearly eight, and some-times he cried in the school yard when the sun went away, cried and ran home, afraid his mother had not returned safely from work. Sometimes, not always. He was good at basketball and the other boys liked him, but they looked at him like a stranger when he cried.

". . . and Jesus is with our boys who are fighting. They write me, some of them I've taught, and they tell me how much they need Jesus, and they know Jesus is with them. The ones who were faithful to him in school are the ones who write the happiest letters." Her hands went up and she spoke between them to the ceiling and she said, "God have mercy on our boys. God have mercy."

In the priests' garage there was a car, a long green car, and the priest with a voice like the man who gave the news on the radio, he owned that car, it was his own car. And the priest, when he crossed the school yard and saw Martin put one in the basket, clapped his hands loudly and said, "Keep shooting, boy." Always the same. "Keep shooting."

The school yard was a large black square except where it was painted white for basketball, and Martin played after school until it was time for his mother to be home from work or until he cried. Sometimes the bigger boys' elbows pumped down on his mouth or ear and he had to go to the side and hold himself where it stung, but he didn't cry, not for that he didn't.

"It is for us they're fighting and some of them will give their lives like Jesus. When you stop to think of it, how beautiful it is. Have any of you here ever thought what a sacrifice it is to give up your life for someone else? As Jesus did? As our boys are doing? Have you?"

One by one hands went up until many hands were up. Martin didn't put up his hand and neither did three or four of the girls, but all of the other boys put up their hands.

She said, "Martin, I'm surprised."

He said nothing. He rarely spoke.

She said, "Quite surprised."

He smiled at her and shook his head, apologizing, and then he looked out the window.

There was smoke coming out of the garage now. He could not see the big roll-down door for he was facing the side of the garage but was sure the door was open because he could see the smoke. It was bluish smoke and it was smoke from the green car unless it was smoke from the car of the priest who looked like a boy. That priest had a car smaller than the green car and not as beautiful.

"What are you looking at, Martin?"

She caught him by surprise, for he thought she was no longer looking. But he told her the truth. He told her he was looking at the smoke.

When he said "smoke" all the children looked. It was a cold day and the smoke held together and went white as it rose, going to puffs turning to streamers, brilliant white and was very pretty. Martin had looked to see the smoke and then the green car when it came out of the garage and the priest in the green car. Now everyone was looking.

The nun had been speaking hard but now she spoke softly and said, "Martin, are you waiting for Father Devlin to appear? Is that it?"

Again he told the truth, by nodding, nothing more.

She said, "I should reprimand you for not paying attention." She smiled and all her teeth, which were large teeth, seemed to show. She said, "But I won't. I think I understand." She looked about. She said, "It seems a lot of boys have made Father Devlin their favorite. Is that true?"

Martin turned to see all of the boys' hands go up along with his own. He glanced back to see if the green car had started into the broad driveway, where it would go around the holly bush and then out to the street; it hadn't. He turned to the nun, not wanting her to speak to him again about looking at the smoke.

"Do any of you know what Father Devlin did before coming to St. Francis?"

A boy's hand went up at the back. The boy was David and had a very deep voice and was taller than Martin or anyone else in the class. He had taught Martin how to shoot a basket over his shoulder. He said, "Wasn't he a chaplain?"

"That's very right," said the nun. "He was indeed a chaplain. He was a chaplain with our troops." She waited and looked down at them, looked back and forth across the classroom at all the faces, and when her eyes landed on Martin he smiled into them. "A chaplain," she said, "and he saw many men die." Again she waited and again she looked. There had been many little noises from the children fidgeting and rolling pencils and playing with ink wells, but after she mentioned the priest having been a chaplain and seeing men dying there weren't any noises.

She said, "Father was near the battlefield and said Mass every morning, and some of the men he said Mass for didn't come back in the afternoon, and that hurt him terribly but it was his reward to know they had heard God and partaken of the Holy Sacrifice before making their own final and supreme sacrifices. Oh, if only he would, the stories Father could tell you!"

She surveyed the faces again. There wasn't even a twitch. All were waiting for more. She smiled at them waiting. She smiled and fixed her glasses on her long nose and closed her eyes and raised her head and seemed to be thinking and when she lowered it she said, "Does anyone know why Father left the war and joined us?"

She waited and waited as though having a contest to see if someone would guess or maybe sneeze or drop a pencil or do something that might trigger an answer, but no one did, and so she said it: "He was wounded." It was a whisper but a heavy whisper all of them could hear. "He went into battle to be with the boys and one day he was wounded."

There was a low appreciative moan. One boy uttered, "Gee!" It was almost "Geeze!" The nun had warned them not to say "Geeze." "Geeze" was short for "Jesus" and it was blasphemy. Martin watched the boy who almost said it and the boy was grinning embarrassed the way someone grins when he almost does something wrong but catches himself. Martin bent down and grinned with the boy, in sympathy with the boy, but the nun did not ask him what he had said, did not make

28

sure it was all right. She was more interested in telling them about the priest and the war.

Martin did want to hear more about the priest and how he was wounded. He wanted more than ever to see the priest. He thought of taking a chance and turning once more, to look at the smoke, but he didn't.

"He was given a medal by the general," she said slowly, and after pausing she added, "The officers and boys in his brigade took up a collection for him after he was wounded." Again she paused. "When he got back to this country, he found something waiting for him, a gift from those he had served." Once more a pause, and then: "Martin, can you guess what the soldiers gave him in appreciation for what he had done for them and their dead comrades?"

Martin gazed up at her. Why had she asked him? He did not know why and did not find out for the answer to her question had begun to throb through him and when he recognized it all else seemed quite clear and he knew it was only right that she ask him, inevitable, as was the answer itself: "A . . . a car. They gave him a car."

"Exactly! How bright of you, Martin!"

The other children turned in admiration but he didn't see them for he was stunned, almost stunned, by his own answer which was pristine and like a needle piercing everything, the spotless blue sky and the face of the nun and the smoke, the pretty smoke outside.

"He came back wounded and found the car waiting for him. He had done so much! And in appreciation the bishop gave him his choice of whatever parish he wanted and he chose ours. How fortunate we are! How very fortunate!"

Most of the students nodded but Martin did not nod for he was no longer listening. He had felt himself shooting up the immense needle to the very top of the universe where he imagined himself, in total darkness, holding on. It was magnificent, and frightening!

"What did you say, David?"

Martin had remained at the top of the needle and had heard David's voice and it had alerted him and he had listened. Now the nun's words were flying up to him through the darkness. Martin listened. It seemed terribly important that he hear, as if David's question, or the answer to it might be his only release from the needle.

"Where was he wounded, Sister?"

Martin opened his eyes, waited.

The nun looked down from the platform on which her desk rested and she looked at the tall boy David and she didn't speak for a few moments and when she did she spoke hesitantly. "It wasn't the same kind of wound you think of . . . when you think of soldiers being wounded. It was . . . ." She looked at her hands on the desk. She looked at the children. "It was a wound all right, a real wound, but . . . ." She raised her hands and opened them before her face as she sometimes did, to slap them together over a hovering fly, only now she didn't slap them together. She gazed between them, "How can I say it?" She remained still, as though the world had suddenly gone to ice and caught her where she was. She was silent and motionless for a long time. When finally words issued from her broad mouth they came in a strange haunted basso like the muted beats of a dirge. "It was . . . it was a wound. It was a terrible wound . . . ." Her hands came down slowly and her face went, twisting, into pain.

All eyes held her, waiting, as if they, the eyes themselves, knew she wasn't finished.

She looked at them, the children's eyes, then knew, or seemed to know: "I . . . I can't tell you." It was a naked whisper: "I can't explain."

She went from religion to arithmetic very quickly, ignoring small grumbles from several of the boys.

It was at the end of the arithmetic lesson that David stood and shouted: "Look!"

Martin turned and saw David standing and pointing out the window, his finger shaking.

Martin looked. The smoke was gone. The boyish priest was kicking wildly and he kicked again and again and then he reached down and tugged at something and Martin knew it was the handle near the bottom but the door didn't open and the breeze flapped through his cassock and he rose up and hammered at the door but it didn't open and then a fat woman Martin recognized as the priests' housekeeper came out of the house and she was wearing an apron with flowers on it and the young priest spoke to her and she reached down and helped him pull at the door but still it didn't open. In the distance Martin could hear them calling, "Father! Father!"

"Close the blinds!" The nun had stood and was waving her arms and shouting, shouting first at David in the back and then at all of them. "Close the blinds!"

Nobody moved.

She came swishing off her platform and stumbled to the first blind and grabbed the string and pulled hard. "Close them in back! Close them this minute!"

No one moved.

She leaped to the second blind and yanked it down. "Close them!" she screamed.

No one seemed to hear.

"You don't understand!" She banged her leg on the radiator going for the third, the blind opposite Martin, and she groaned but went on and got the string and pulled and the blind flew down with a ripping sound, stayed.

But Martin had seen. He had seen the young priest take the handle, had seen him pull against it with his life, had seen the door burst open, had seen the priest and the woman surrounded by a mountain of smoke.

She stumbled on but did not reach the back window in time. David shouted. David said, "They're carrying him out!"

31

Philip F. O'Connor

"Stop it, David!"

David said, "They're pulling him on the ground and his coat is up! I can see his shirt and his stomach is sticking out! They're pulling him toward the holly bush!"

"David!"

"They've gone past the holly bush!"

She reached up and her hand snapped at the string of David's blind and she brought it down, slashing down, and she turned on David and spoke fiercely to him through teeth that were yellow and tight: "Be silent, you cur!" She stood before him and glared at him until he sat down. She raised her eyes. "Be silent! All of you!"

And they were.

My Imaginary Father

One night, in his bedroom at the tail of a binge, my father began to talk about his headstone, a little slab of concrete to be placed flat on the grass near potter's field in Holy Cross Cemetery. He had mentioned the headstone at other times, but now told me there would be an epitaph. Flipping his hand up, thumb and forefinger about an inch apart, he spoke it out, slashing the air for each of its lines:

HERE LIE THE BONES
OF
AN ANGRY MAN
NO SON OF THE GOLDEN WEST

He struggled out of his pants and searched the top of his bed until he found the wooden coat hanger for which he'd been looking. "With an exclamation mark at the end: 'West!'"

I nodded.

"Maybe I'd better write it down."

"I'll remember."

"Demons!" He placed his pants over the bar at the bottom of the hanger, then held the hanger out, him swaying this way and the hanger that, until, fussing with the pants, he had them right, cuffs to waist. "Traitors!" He weaved to the closet and snapped the hanger onto the clothes rack. He unbuttoned his shirt, removed it, turned and put it on the hanger over his pants, managing, after several tries to get the top button closed. "Exploiters!" He returned to the bed, tucking his underwear tops into his boxer shorts. He stopped and looked at me. "Well, I've put you in charge," he said sharply. "If there are any questions you'd better ask them now."

"I don't have any."

He lowered himself into the bed, pulling the blankets up until only the bright dome of his head, his fierce dark eyes and long bone of a nose showed over the top. He lay there thinking. His eyes descended to mine. "They might try to have it scratched off. If they do that you'd better be prepared to stand up to them. There are laws against tampering with a man's grave. Remember that."

I told him I would. "Is there anything else?"

He closed his eyes. "Nothing."

I switched off the light, backed out of the room and closed the door behind me.

In the kitchen my mother had been rattling about, but apparently she'd heard every word. She snatched up the broom, which stood just inside the back door, and began to sweep. "A headstone! Isn't that a luxurious thing to be thinking about at a time like this?" Sweep sweep. The broom seemed to be picking up nothing. "And what happens when my back goes to pieces?" She had been complaining of a low back pain for several months. It seemed to get worse when he was drinking. She went to the corner and bent over with a groan, picking up the dust pan. When she rose it fell from her hand with a clatter. I went over, picked it up, then knelt in front of her while she pushed in the handful of scraps she'd managed to get. She snapped the pan away from me, crossed the room and flipped the contents into a large paper bag on the floor beside the sink. She put the broom against the wall, dropped the pan noisily to the floor beside it, then shuffled to the window.

Her eyes drifted out, over the neighbors' scrubby back yards, past the gray back walls of the stores on the town's main street, across to the scarred face of Red Hill, up, into the darkening sky, where a handful of stars hung scattered, aloof, eons apart, gazing blindly back at her. She turned. "What have they ever done to him?"

I shook my head. I had no answer. There was none as far as I could tell. As his drinking had increased so had his talk about his enemies. Lately there was only one.

She lowered her eyes and began to work on the few dishes that remained in the sink, asking me to help her. I did so.

Later I returned to his bedroom, where I opened the door and looked in at him. He was snoring thunderously. In the light from the hall I could see his head hanging over the side, his mouth open in a misshapen oval: a soldier who'd been shot going to his foxhole. I thought of easing his head back onto the pillow, but I didn't, afraid to wake him.

I went to my bedroom, changed and got into bed. I lay awake, waiting to hear a thump on the floor. Sometimes he fell. When that happened he cursed. The cursing let us know he wasn't hurt. One of us, my mother or I, would go in and help him up. I stayed awake for about an hour but he didn't fall.

The pattern of his drinking had changed. Once he had needed Uncle Dave or one of our San Francisco relatives as an alibi. Lately, however, he began without excuses and at the oddest times: Tuesday mornings, Thursday afternoons. He'd start for work with a suit or tie on but march right past the bus depot and end up at Henry's Tavern. Or, making it to work, he'd call from the city in the middle of an afternoon with something about a changed bus schedule or a friend at work with a terrible personal problem to talk over. ("And what," my mother said after one of his calls, "does his friend think he has?")

35

If he did make it through the week sober, he was likely to fall on the weekend. One Saturday afternoon recently he'd gone into the yard to water the quince he'd once planted—it never seemed to grow—and a few minutes later I looked out the window to see the hose beside the tree with water dribbling out of it, but no waterer. And no longer did he return from Henry's to creep into his underground, our basement, like a stalking cat, there to sip his way toward a hangover with the contraband whiskey he kept hidden (in label-less cans, old vinegar bottles, preserve jars and other suspicious containers), but instead came up the stairs with a roar, a bear out of a nightmare, ranting about his enemy. There had always been enemies, old personal ones like Monsignor Rock, our pastor; Buckley, the grocer; and Berner, his supervisor at the phone company. Also monumental ones: The Church, The Government, The Bank, Women. But these he'd recently abandoned. He had fixed on an organization called *The Loyal Sons and Daughters of the Golden West*. It was the *Sons and Daughters* he had referred to in the bedroom.

To me the group seemed innocent enough, descendants of California pioneers whose main activity each year was a lavish ball given to raise money for (one of my father's lesser nemeses) Charity. Long standing suspicions had been confirmed after he spent a sober weekend reading California history from some books he took out of the town library. Afterwards he concluded that the ancestors had been pioneers all right, but pioneers only in crime. He had apparently read between the lines. Far from civilizing the state as the descendants and some of the historians claimed, they had butchered the Indians and plundered their land; had been among the state's notorious shanghai-artists, vigilantes and gold grabbers; and had later built robber-baron empires not only on the blood and bones of the Indians but also of the Chinese and (worst of all) the Irish. History was history and might have been left in its grave if, over a period of weeks, he hadn't managed to enmesh the past and the present. As he saw it, the guilt of the ancestors, swollen by years of no-restitution, had traveled down the decades and now lay heavily on the descendants. I tried to argue with him, particularly with his logic, but it did no good. Nothing seemed to do any good. When talking about the *Sons and Daughters* his face would grow florid and he would hiss and fume and squeeze soft objects that lay within hand's reach. If he was drunk he pranced about with flailing gestures that made it seem as though he were fighting off invisible hands pulling at him, trying to fling him out a window or through a doorway. I sat like a mute, listening, ready to leap up and prevent him from going to the floor or down the basement stairs. I was sure that if he fell he would suffer one of those painfully serious injuries, like a broken hip, that it took months and months to cure. He always managed to stay on his feet, however, raging on until, tired from the whiskey or the talk, he'd find his way to his bedroom, where, if I were still with him, he'd continue talking about the enemy until he had changed and tucked himself under the blankets.

Recently someone at the phone company, perhaps someone who had had to listen to him go on about the *Sons and Daughters,* had prankishly slipped a letter into his inside coat pocket. He found it when he got home from work, the letterhead showing it was from the San Francisco headquarters of the organization. He opened the envelope, removed the letter and read aloud:

> Here it is, time to plan our annual "Pow Wow" and we find our "tribal" funds a little low. We know how much our traditional fund-raiser means to the public in the Bay Area and so we must call on you, our friends, for support. Remember! All proceeds go to the Needy! As in the past . . . .

Philip F. O'Connor

His eyes jumped up in amazement. He threw the letter on the kitchen table. He looked at it. He picked it up again and read silently. He threw it on the floor and started to kick it toward the stove. He hesitated, picked it up and read once more. "I don't believe this." He began to tear it into small pieces. When he had all the pieces cupped in one hand he opened the lid on the burner with the other and threw them in. He turned around, looked at my mother. "The people's money," he whispered. But that was all. He soared out of the kitchen. I thought he might be headed for Henry's, but he wasn't; the letter had apparently taken too much out of him. He sat in the living room all evening, mumbling low like a car warming up down the street. He didn't start drinking until the next morning. The binge that followed lasted five days.

My mother made me his guardian then. It was a sign of her growing desperation. At eleven years old, she felt, I could do what she couldn't, keep a close eye on him. Keeping close eye on him meant I had to follow him to Henry's to make sure he didn't stumble or lose his way or get picked up by a local policeman. (He knew most of the town's policemen and on my second night on duty I saw him encounter one, a pudgy patrolman named Sam, whom he put his arm around and took into Henry's with him. He stayed all evening. For all I know, Sam stayed, having his ears filled with the nefarious exploits of the *Sons and Daughters*.) I was also supposed to watch him around the house and yard, whether he was drunk or sober. My mother had instructed me to get his mind, in one subtle way or another, off both the enemy and drink. I had no subtle ways, and I resented the assignment, not only because I was no good at it but also because it kept me away from baseball games, hikes and swimming excursions with my seventh-grade classmates. Above all, I had no interest in an organization that had nothing to do with my life, or, from all I could tell, his.

38

He survived the letter and remained peaceful until he saw the newspaper article announcing the ball. "Well," he said, nodding, "they've gotten what they want after all." He must have been doing a great deal of thinking, for immediately he announced that he had it all figured out. "A trick," he said, "a trick on the people!" He began to tramp through the house, nodding, mumbling, answering invisible conversants: "It's no excuse! You've declared yourselves now!" He finally returned to the kitchen table and struck his hand once, and very hard, on its surface. "There's one you haven't fooled, murderers!"

With that began his latest and worst binge, the one that was now, hopefully, coming to an end. It was the worst because of his incredible threats. He saw nothing wrong, he told me the first or second night, with putting a bomb under the ballroom where the *Sons and Daughters'* dance was being held. "Not that I'd do it, mind you. I'm speaking only of the morality of the thing." Bombs turned to lawsuits and lawsuits to petitions, none of which he'd done a thing about. But it was clear to both my mother and me that he was getting close to the possible, at least for him.

My mother recalled fretfully that several years earlier, when I was six or seven, he had tried to place a long distance call to President Roosevelt to demand the release of the Nisei from Tule Lake, a camp where they had been incarcerated for the duration of World War II. He couldn't get through and was planning another call when she talked him out of it, reminding him that Uncle Dave was soon due for a visit and that he and Dave might be able to figure out a better solution together. It was an old tactic. She hoped that his plan would dissipate when their attention became fixed totally on drinking. But when Dave arrived his plan merely grew. I remembered the afternoon when they decided to go themselves to Tule Lake in Dave's Model A, cut the barbed wire around the camp and lead the Nisei to freedom:

39

"If Ireland had bombed Pearl Harbor, we'd now be locked up too," Dave said.

"Absolutely! They're true-blue immigrants, as innocent as us!" My mother claimed later that it was only God's good grace that kept my father from finding his hedge clippers and Dave from being able to locate Tule Lake on a map. No matter. For days they went on talking about the daring raid and only dropped the subject when my father said the camp was probably guarded and they'd no doubt be shot going in.

"Well that puts an end to that," Dave said sensibly. I had enjoyed hearing the two of them boast about things that, even then, I was pretty sure they wouldn't do. Then and later, my father, encouraged by Dave or whiskey, seemed able to shoulder mountains into the sea. Even as time passed and I saw him do nothing heroic, there remained the unspeakable threats and magnificent curses: fumes, clouds, words. Justice seemed to have been served merely in the act of talking.

"Well, his head seems to be screwed tightly back on now," my mother said with revived hope when I came in from Sunday Mass the following morning.

I thought she might be right. He was sitting quietly in the living room reading the *Examiner*. Silence and immobility were signs of recovery. With a day of rest there was a chance he'd be back to work on Monday morning. I remained hopeful until I went to the living room after breakfast to get the sports section.

All of the newspaper sections were on his lap and he held the top one open and was bent forward, peering into it like a scientist examining something fantastic that had just swum under his microscope. He scratched above his ear, making the soft darkish hair stick out, then shook his head and began to mumble. I stood before him for several minutes before he noticed me:

"What do *you* want?"

I told him.

He flipped through the sections beneath the top one, ripping the sports section from the pile, holding it out to me.

When I sat down on the sofa, I saw him drop his head and continue with whatever it was he'd been looking at. He went on mumbling as I glanced at the baseball scores. Finally he smacked his hand on the open page before him and looked up. He was wearing the astonished expression of someone who'd just been slapped in the face by a stranger. "By! Holy! Jesus!" he said to no one. "That does it!" He flung the section he'd been reading under the big radio next to his chair where—schwack!— it broke apart in a splash of white. He leaped up, made a quick check of his back pocket and thundered toward the front door.

When the door shut I rushed across the room and found the section he'd been reading. In a moment I recognized the offensive pages. Under a large script headline —*A Gathering of Tribes*—a lot of drunk looking people grinned out from the photographs. All of them wore Indian costumes, though none of them seemed to be Indians. Some of the women were slim and pretty while most of the men were old and paunchy. Single and double feathers stuck out of the women's elaborate hairdos and several of the men wore long chiefs' bonnets. All the faces were painted grotesquely, with circles, stripes, spots and the like. There were bows, quivers, beads, necklaces and gaudy moccasins. Trinkets, icons and miniature totems surrounded the rest. More noticeable than all the decorations, however, were the celebrants themselves, their odd faces, their hairy legs and bumpy knees. I let the paper fall to the floor and started for the kitchen, certain now that the *Loyal Sons and Daughters* owned my father.

When I told my mother what had happened, she collapsed into one of the kitchen chairs and began to cry. At certain times there was just no way to deal with her. She prayed and sobbed through the rest of the morning, so forlorn that I decided to cancel plans for a hike on Mount Baldy with several of my friends. At one point, like a religious zealot, she got down on the floor and sobbed out a decade of the rosary. When she stood, she asked if I thought she ought to call Monsignor Rock and ask him to go over to Henry's and try to pull him out. I knew how my father felt about the pastor, and, picturing him impulsively opening his hand and catching the priest on the side of his soft red race, I gave her a firm no. She moaned and wailed and talked about the curse of the Irish and the damnation of fools. She finally got the *Alcoholics Anonymous* booklet she kept hidden in her clothespin bag. She flipped through it, looking for guidance, but didn't find any. She sank again into a state of desperation, coming out of it only when she recalled an old and not very reliable solution:

"Jackie," she said. "You'll just have to go over and bring him back."

My trips to Henry's had taught me something about the quality of the place. It had a changing personality. On Saturday nights, for example, there was a lot of movement and a lot of noise. The one time I had gone to rescue my father on a Saturday night I had had a hard time even spotting him. Because of the shouting and the music and the bodies passing back and forth in front of me, I couldn't keep my eyes focused on a single object or person for more than a few seconds. After peeking between legs and around torsos I was about to leave, thinking he wasn't there, when through a crack in the blur, I saw a familiar hand at the bar go shooting out, out and down, toward the ample bottom of a passing waitress. I then heard a blast of laughter and a carefree shout, both unmistakable: "I missed!" I stepped forward and saw his eyes circling drunkenly, then his enormous grin. "Get her next time around," he said loudly, turning to his companion at the bar, a mechanic who worked at the garage at the end of town. Embarrassed, I backed out through the door, not wanting him to see me, not wanting anyone to know I was his son.

Sundays, fortunately, were different. The customers on Sundays, a handful, sat apart from each other like strangers at a train station, their mesmerized eyes held on objects far across the room. They moved hardly at all, ordering drinks from Henry by delicate movements of fingers or wrists or maybe the steady tapping of an empty glass on the table. They rarely spoke. Even Henry (who must have weighed 300 pounds) seemed barely able to respond to the orders. The lights were dim and he, all of them, looked like ghosts, frozen or in slow motion. It was usually easy to get my father's attention, to let him know I was there.

I pushed open the leather-lined door and saw him on a bar stool near the cash register, turned all the way around, holding or seeming to hold the attention of perhaps a dozen glazed eyes:

"Does no one care? Is *that* it?"

There wasn't a flicker of response, neither enthusiasm nor disgust. The others, mostly old men, were simply present, observing something that, at this unlikely time of the day and week, was in front of them, gesturing and making noise.

"Or maybe you don't understand what I'm driving at?"

Not a sound. Not a move.

"Did none of you read the society section of the *Examiner* this morning?"

Nothing.

"Damn it!" he said, turning to face Henry, a puzzled blob who had been gazing at his back, wrinkling one side of his face each time my father had asked a question, as if trying to understand the momentous nature of his statements. "There's something got to be done about

43

Philip F. O'Connor

them!" He searched Henry's eyes, hopeful. "Did you read the paper?"

Henry frowned, apologizing, and shook his head.

"A disgrace! That's all it is."

I stood just inside the door, wanting and not wanting to run. Had the present binge not lasted as long as it had, had there not been so many binges recently, I might have slipped out and let him rant away until he had the others believing in him which I was sure he was able to do. But I was angry. He had missed a week of work, and the pay that went with it. Because of him my mother seemed to be losing her mind. I myself had been robbed of one more afternoon with my friends. I wanted him to come home. That was the important thing, maybe only a beginning, but the important thing, and I said it. From a few feet inside the doorway I called across, "Why don't you come home?"

He turned. At first his wet uncertain eyes seemed not to believe I was even there. I had come in at other times but rarely spoken, never called out, just let him see me and, in seeing me, get my mother's message: she wanted him to return. Then I'd flee, hoping he'd follow.

"What's this?"

"What do they have to do with you?"

"What do they have to do with me?" He turned his surprised face to Henry, as if now, at last, Henry had an answer for him. He turned quickly back. "Who?" he demanded.

"Those *Sons and Daughters.* Why do you care about them?" I could hear my voice rising. It cracked before I finished, my last words coming out like a girl's. "They've never hurt you." I thought the others might laugh but they didn't.

I saw the blood simmering under my father's eyes. I think the others, their presence, kept him in control, kept the blood from spilling down his cheeks as it often did when he was raging about the *Sons and Daughters.*

44

Abruptly a scratchy voice sounded from the corner. "A chip off the old block, eh, John?"

He gave a quick nod of recognition, but his eyes remained on me, searing me, as if they were trying to penetrate my skin, burn through and find the real me. Then, little by little, they went around me as if he might capture what he was looking for in the air. I thought he'd start yelling, but he didn't. All he said, flatly, was "Hurt me," almost questioning. He picked up the shot glass before him and flung the contents into his mouth. All the muscles of his face suddenly dove inward, toward an invisible point somewhere under his nose. He wiggled his mouth and nose. When the muscles went back to normal, he gave his head a little snap, sign of survival, and looked at me.

Henry had been watching me too, giving me fat smiles. Once, out of habit I suppose, he raised the *Early Times* bottle from under the counter, about to offer my father another shot, but then he looked at me and lowered it, as if, after all these years, he realized someone knew he'd been poisoning the town's population.

Finally my father spoke. "We're going to have a talk, you and I."

"Now?"

"Later." He pushed the shot glass aside and got off his stool. "We're leaving now."

I thought he'd clout the back of my head when we got outside. He'd done that now and then when I was younger. He didn't. He told me to walk in front of him. I did so, silent, not daring to pull at willow branches or kick stones or do anything else that might further anger him. He made me stay in front of him all the way. When we got to the bottom of the front steps, he said, "I'm going to take a nap. Call me in an hour."

"To talk?"

"In an hour," he said, going ahead of me up the stairs.

45

Inside he went directly to his bedroom, shutting the door behind him.

In the kitchen my mother, stunned by the quickness with which I'd gotten him home, said, "You're a miracle worker, Jackie. I don't know how you did it."

I didn't either. And I didn't feel like a miracle worker. I told her I'd done nothing except challenge him about the *Sons and Daughters*. She was shaking her head, still impressed.

I called him in time for supper. During the meal none of us spoke. My mother took extra care putting down and picking up things in front of him, not wanting to upset a delicate balance between sobriety and drunkenness. I tried to avoid his eyes, afraid I might tempt him to start snapping at me about something. He himself, his clothes wrinkled, his face ashen and serious, ate quickly and didn't utter a sound until he was finished eating. Then he turned to me and said, "When you're ready there, Jackie, we'll take a little walk, maybe up to that hill you like so much."

His inviting tone eased my fears, but my mother looked at him apprehensively, supposing, I think, that he'd found another ploy to get himself back to Henry's.

He seemed to notice. He said, reassuring her, "Just a walk. Just a little walk."

Red Hill blocked the highway at the north end of town. At the foot of the hill the highway forked to the left, winding toward Fairfax and the other small towns in the hilly, wooded country that divided the town from the coast, about thirty miles away, and to the right toward San Rafael, flatly along a straight road that eventually connected with the main north-south highway to San Francisco. From the top of the hill the view was magnificent: commanding mountains to the south, the richly dark hills and hazy valleys to the west and to the east the bay, blue and expansive, with cities clustered

whitely on the slopes beyond it. I went to the top of Red
Hill often, usually in late afternoon, and spent a lot of
time looking out. Below me the town was like a painted
village, something I had projected onto the framework
of the rest, my own ongoing creation. When I saw a car
or a puff of smoke or maybe a previously unnoticed cottage, I imagined I had just put it there with a quick dap-
pling stroke, as if it were my fate to complete a picture
that was ever-moving, ever-changing, but could never
really be finished. Darkness came surprisingly fast, and
when it did I would get up, find one of the flattened cardboard boxes I or another boy had left beside a tree or
against a large rock, then rush home, hoping I wasn't
late for supper.

When we left the house he made no effort to keep me
in front of him. The cool evening breeze seemed to
awaken and cheer him. I was grateful. Often, when he
slept after drinking, he would wake up sour and jumpy.
Now he walked briskly and I had to hurry to keep up.
When we got to the bottom of the hill, he said, "Do you
want to race to the top?"

The challenge took me by surprise. I did not even race
my friends to the top of the hill, for it was difficult
enough, digging hands and feet into the red clay beneath
the grass, to get oneself up. How could he, so much older,
a man of little exercise, wheezing now (the way he did
after a lot of drinking), hope to beat me to the top? I
told him it might be better if we climbed together.

"Nonsense." He cut across the level patch at the bottom and started up, not going on all fours directly, as I
usually did, but sideclimbing, zigzagging across again,
all with surprising swiftness.

I remained at the bottom watching, impressed.

About twenty yards up he turned, looked back, saw I
hadn't started yet, and said, "What's the matter, Jackie?
Afraid of a little contest?"

I started then, doing it my own way, the only way I

knew how. Soon, clawing at the hill, I was moving swiftly. I glanced about, hoping I'd passed him. In the growing darkness I couldn't see him, so I kept moving, trying to go faster. In a couple of minutes, when I was about to look for him again, I heard his voice from somewhere above, laughing. I looked up but still couldn't see him. Challenged, I dug in harder, my arms and legs churning. The laughter grew louder. There was nothing to do but keep going, hoping that in the darkness I would get past him. I finally reached the large rock near the top, the one on which I often sat. I dropped down, panting, and again looked around. There was no sign of him, and I thought maybe I had, after all, passed him. But then his voice sounded, from above and behind me:

"What did you do, stop for a little snooze?"

I spun around.

He stood between two of several tall trees at the very top. One hand was resting easily against the trunk of one of the trees. His tieless white shirt shone, almost luminescently, in the dim light reflected upward from the town. Again he laughed. I squinted and finally made out his eyes, glistening as they moved, taking the scene below us. He stayed at the top for a while, then came down and stood beside the rock on which I was sitting:

"I can see why you like to come up here."

I nodded, "How did you get up so fast?"

"I'm an old hill-climber from way back," he said lightly, sitting down beside me. He picked up a handful of tall grass, plucked out a few bits of weed, shook it, then began to wind it over the palm of his left hand, making it flow, supply, like threads of silk. He gazed out for a while, then said, "A good place to dream. Am I right?"

"Yes." He seemed to have caught perfectly the meaning of the hill to me. It was one of those unusual moments when his thoughts and mine seemed to have coincided. I wondered if he too had looked out, seen something that, at the moment of seeing, he pretended he had put there.

"You were curious about something there in Henry's this afternoon. Why I feel the way I do about those . . . those blackguards. You want a quick answer, I suppose." Before I could tell him that's not what I wanted, he went on. "There's no quick answer. In fact it has a lot to do with the passage of time, figuring out the likes of them. It has to do with a lot of things."

Sometimes he'd get to a point by going around it first. I supposed he was doing that now.

"The country, for example. When I was a child I used to dream about this country. That's a laugh, isn't it?"

I didn't think it was. "I don't understand."

"And how could you?" He flung the grass out into the breeze, which quickly caught it, blew it apart and tossed it back at him. He brushed some of it off his shirt and said, "How could you when I didn't? It's part of being Irish. We're suckers, most of us, we let ourselves be taken for an awful ride, those of us who came over from the old country. We more than others. Subject to dreams is why. And most of us purchased the dreams they had to offer, lock, stock and barrel. It's always been that way. Do you remember the ones I told you about immigrating in the last century?"

"The ones that were crowded into the boats?"

"That's right. No matter where they were bound for, Boston or New York or wherever, there wasn't a one of 'em, not a one, no matter if they were suffering from scurvy or pneumonia, I'm sure there wasn't one who didn't, even in his dying gasps, give up the hope they would make it to the other side and, more important, that there would be others there on the dock with baskets of food and maybe a band playing and God-knows-what-else. Not for a moment did they give up, being who they were. You can put your money on that. Dreamers. Like children the way they believed, and they kept coming, shipload after shipload. For what?"

He'd talked about the Irish immigrants earlier. After they arrived some stayed in the big cities and took slavish jobs, as janitors, washer-women, trolley conductors, working until they died, old too early, almost always poor. Others had gone on, to Canada, the West, elsewhere, but whether they stayed in the cities or helped build railroads and factories and highways, the results were very much the same. With rare exception it was a lifetime of hard work with little or nothing to show for it. His answer was built into his question he'd asked me, which may have been why he didn't wait for me to give it.

"The rest of us, the ones who came later, should have learned from them. But we didn't. Over we came, convincing ourselves it would be different." He lowered his head and scratched above his ear, always a sign of thought. "I suppose it was the stories that this one or that one had made a fortune that hooked us. Just enough temptation to let us keep on believing it was better on the other side of the water. Damn fools we were, looking back now. Damn fools!" He swung around, as if wanting to catch me by surprise, to check to see if I were listening.

I was.

"So you wonder why I talk about those others, the so-called *Sons and Daughters*. Well, I'll tell you why. They're the ones who not only had it from the start but who could have reached down and helped the others, made it come true for them. Why didn't they? Eh?" Not waiting for the answer he didn't want anyway, he kicked at a large stone sticking out of the ground in front of him, kicked several times but didn't quite uproot it. "Charity balls. That's the best they can do," he said, giving a last futile kick. "Always has been. They've had time to know better. They've hidden behind their wealth, not letting themselves realize there are still thousands, millions, in bad shape in the world, Irish and Black men and Jews and Indians and God-knows-what-else, not knowing it's going to take a lot more than charity balls to cure the ills their sort has caused." Once more he shoved his foot against the stone, this time getting it in at the side for a foothold. He grunted, trying to shove it out. It didn't work. "God forgive me, but I'd become a . . . ." Again he shoved at the stone; nothing. ". . . a Bolshevik if I was younger, get the rest to come along. Let the others stop us if they could." Whack! He had drawn his leg back and given a tremendous kick. The stone tumbled out of place, remaining loose next to its socket. He looked at it, still occupied with what he was saying. "It's simply not right, them having servants and big cars and summer places when others are trying to find a simple pot to pee in. It's as wrong as anything I know." Now, with a simple nudge, he sent the stone tumbling down the hill, noisily through the tall grass until, somewhere near the bottom, it slowed and came to a stop. "I've measured the dream, Jackie, and it doesn't come to much." His voice was lower now, the heft of his anger having been spent. "I've woken up, and I've found myself with enemies. I'm afraid there's no choice." He stood, turned and looked down at me. "That's something you might learn from what I've said. There are still enemies to be fought. Still wars to be fought. Inescapable. That you can bet on." He stopped, looked around puzzled, and said, "How do you get down off this blasted hill?"

I told him I used one of the flattened cardboard boxes buried under the branches and twigs a few yards away, but I suggested that, since it was dark now, we could take the winding path that went down the back, less steep, part of the hill. No, he said, the box would be fine; he hadn't done anything like that in a long time: "We'll make another race of it." I crossed the hill, wondering at my own uneasiness about the things he'd been doing and saying. The race to the top had seemed impossible, yet he'd beaten me. His antagonism toward the *Loyal*

Sons and Daughters had earlier made little sense, but now it seemed part of a complete philosophy of life, worked out and even consistent. The pieces were coming together. Still, I was nervous about him wanting to race down. I didn't know why. I picked out two fast-looking boxes and brought them back, warning him about the fence posts at the bottom, just where the hill began to level out.

"Jump off if you see yourself headed for one because you can't turn these things."

"I'll take care of myself," he said, and he seated himself on the front of his box, hunching forward.

I watched him peer ahead like a race driver looking through his windshield. He glanced down once. The hill looked much steeper from the top than from the bottom. His eyes widened momentarily, then he turned to me, seated on my box beside him, and said, "Who says, 'On your mark, get set, go'?"

"I'll say it."

"Go ahead."

In a moment the lights of the town were splashing before me. At night there was no way to spot rises and pits you could brace yourself for. I hit a rock and almost fell off. I hung tightly onto the sides and kept going. The wind, the bumps, sent me to my back, but I kept holding on. "Whoaaahhh!" Him. He was behind me, and I thought he'd fallen off. I couldn't turn around. The town expanded before me. I tried to see the fence posts; I couldn't. The speed was fantastic. I heard myself cry out for the speed. "With you, Jackaieee!" This time much closer. Just as I heard him I struck something and tumbled off, somersaulting down, twisting off to one side, then sliding, slowing, stopping. I raised my head and looked toward the fence posts about thirty yards down the hill. I expected to see him there, waiting.

"Ai, Jackie!" It came from above.

I turned around and saw him about ten yards behind me.

"That damn thing slipped out or I would have passed you." I saw him stand, lean into the hill for balance and start down. "You should have told me about the bumps. You didn't mention them. Are you all right?"

"Yes."

He came down the hill laughing. "By God!" he said. "That was some trip!"

We went to the bottom together. He had left his box on the hill. I put mine under a strip of sheet metal near a clump of trees and we started home. He began to rave about the ride once again. "By God!" he said when we crossed the highway near the bus depot, "That was fun!" He repeated the statement, or a variation, a couple of times before we reached the house. "By God! I don't know when I've had fun like that!" He sounded like one of my cousins from the city after he had come down the hill for the first time. "We'll do it again someday." He wanted to race to the house. We started at the corner of our street. I shot ahead, beating him by a few yards. "I'm getting old, Jackie. That's all it is. Just getting old." He did sound a little old, the way he was heaving to catch his breath, the way the words came drily out of him. I followed him down the walk, then went up the stairs ahead of him and opened the door. He made his way past me to the kitchen, where I heard him say to my mother, "We had quite a time, the two of us."

"Does that mean you'll be back to work in the morning?" she said skeptically.

"What makes you think I wouldn't be?" The water tap went on. The water splashed for a minute or so. I heard him swallowing loudly, like a man that had just crawled across a desert. "Eh?"

She didn't answer.

He went to bed then, telling me once more, as he passed me in the hall, what a great time he'd had.

The following morning I got up early to catch up on some reading for school that I'd missed because of the busy weekend. I found him at the kitchen table looking immaculate in his clean white shirt and freshly pressed pants. He was eating oatmeal. "Sit down there, Jackie," he said, "and tell me what you've got planned for the day." He pointed to the chair beside him.

I sat down and told him: "The same as usual, except for a test in English. On a Washington Irving story I have to read."

"That's the sleeper, isn't it?"

"Well, Rip Van Winkle is. The test is on 'The Legend of Sleepy Hollow.'"

"Yes. That's right. Rip. I read that story in school in Ireland."

I watched him eat.

"I'll tell you," he said finally. "There's a lot in books if you read them the right way, with a point-of-view of your own. Let them change you if they can. But have something in mind when you start." He sipped his coffee and finished the oatmeal.

I asked where my mother was. He said she'd gone to the corner for a bottle of milk. "About that talk we had," he said. "No need to worry her about it. She'll never understand the way I think. She'll never understand about those . . . those jackals."

"I won't tell her," I said quickly, not wanting him to work himself up.

She came in a few minutes later. He had gotten up and spooned himself a second helping of oatmeal. When she put the bottle of milk on the table, he opened it and poured some over the oatmeal.

"Well," she said to him, "do you think you'll make it through the day?"

"And why wouldn't I?" He seemed offended.

I got a bowl out of the cupboard and poured myself some oatmeal. While I was eating my father stopped once and winked at me, a reminder not to go into what we'd talked about the night before. There was no need for the reminder but I nodded anyway. I had no idea why he wanted to keep his ideas from her. They had helped me understand him better; they might have helped her, softened her fears a little. I wasn't going to fight him, however, even inside myself. He had stopped drinking, that was the important thing. He got up and stood by his chair, stretching his arms out, making a loud groaning yawn. "Well, I'll be at the bus in plenty of time. That'll be nice. That'll be nice." He went into the hall to get his coat.

My mother called, "You be sure to check and see if they'll let you count any of those missed days last week on your sick leave."

"Ah, stop worrying," he called back. "I'm still well within my allowance."

She shook her head, knowing it wasn't true. "Check anyway."

He didn't answer. The front door opened.

"Take the umbrella," she said. "I heard on the radio it's raining in the city."

"They're hardly ever right," he answered. "Anyway, I've left it at work." Before she could say anything more he'd closed the door and was gone.

I did not get time to finish the Irving story before leaving for school, but I stayed in the classroom during recess and made it nearly to the end. Sister Imelda gave the test after recess. I did well enough, a "B" I think, considering the short time I'd had to study.

At lunch time we had a game of softball with the eighth grade. I was co-captain of the seventh grade team and played catcher, as usual. The first time I batted I hit a spinning hot grounder that hugged the ground until it struck something in front of their third baseman. He leaped up and made a very good catch just above his head. He also made a good throw but I was running

55

hard and reached first base safely. Turning, waiting for
the pitch to the next batter, I felt suddenly, incredibly,
angry. It took me a couple of pitches to figure it out.
There had been cheers after my hit. But they weren't for
me. I'd hit the ball well. I'd not slowed up when I saw
the third baseman moving in on it. I'd made it to first
safely because I'd run hard. But the third baseman had
made an exceptional catch and the cheers were for him.
Had he fumbled with the ball or had the ball spun past
him, the cheers would have been mine. It *was* a good hit.
I stood on first through two outs, hoping the next batter
would get me around to third. I planned how I would
knock the third baseman down if he tried to tag me. The
next batter popped up, however, and I was left on first.
We won the game by a couple of runs.

Back in the classroom for the afternoon I had a hard
time concentrating. The ponderous answers of some of
my slower-witted classmates to questions on American
history bored and irritated me. Sister was paying special
attention to them, trying to get them caught up. Dopes, I
thought, everything in their heads awkward and stumbling. I leaned back and closed my eyes, imagining my
father in there with me. First, he was being asked questions, and he was snapping back quickly, not just answering either, but interpreting the facts. There was more to
the slavery question than the book, the nun, or my dull
classmates could have seen. He would know. He would
tell them. Then I thought of him as the teacher not having to wait to answer questions, just spilling it out, all
he knew. The class would be interesting with him there;
that was certain. My fantasies wound on until they,
too, began to bore me. I forced myself to listen to the
others, struggling, most of them getting at least a sem-
blance of a right answer after much effort. Sister congratulated them on their improvement.

There was a softball game after school. I skipped it
and went home to help my mother plant carrots and tur-

nips in the little backyard garden she started every spring. She had grown up on a farm in Ireland and it was a pleasure to watch her work, quickly and smoothly, as if she knew every inch of soil by heart. I tried to emulate her movements, work as certainly as she, but I couldn't, and after I had laid down a couple of rows of seeds she had to come over and re-plant several of them. She was exhausted when we finished and she took a nap on the sofa until it was time to start supper.

My father arrived home just before six, on time. "What a day!" he said, coming in, his collar open and his tie slightly loosened. He went directly to the kitchen and poured himself a glass of water. (He must have drunk a gallon each day for weeks after each binge.) When he finished he turned and said, "You'd think someone'd take up the slack when a man misses a few days." He wiped away a few drops of water that had spilled on his chin. "That isn't the way it happens, though. No, sir." He went to the living room but didn't read the newspaper, as he usually did. When I went in after finishing my homework to ask him if he'd like to throw the baseball on the street, he was by the big radio, looking out at the houses and hills to the east, his face hanging a little, hollow at the cheeks. No, he said, he didn't think he wanted to throw the baseball. But maybe tomorrow. He kept looking out, expectant, a spy observing an alien country, waiting for something to happen, an explosion, revolution, something to snap life into him again, something to celebrate, to file in his next report. At supper he asked my mother what she had planted in the garden this year, but as she began to tick off the vegetables he nibbled at his food and didn't seem to hear her. When the meal was finished he went back to the living room but stayed only a short time. On his way to bed he said only, "Work takes a lot out of a man, Jackie."

"The crisis is ended," my mother said later. "I suppose I can have my side of the bed back now."

I nodded in agreement, though I wasn't nearly as certain as she.

He remained quiet until Friday, getting home promptly each evening, usually going to the living room until supper, after which he tinkered in the garden, passively taking orders from my mother ("Those aren't weeds; they're carrots. Leave them alone."), watering his hopeless quince, suggesting a row of sauerkraut beneath the back stairs. ("You don't grow it," she told him. "It comes from cabbage. And anyway there's no sun under the back stairs.") Once he came out on the street and threw hard grounders at me for nearly an hour ("Get that knee down! If you miss with the mitt, the leg'll stop it."), so fiercely, underhanded, the way he must have learned playing hurley in Ireland, that my baseball was full of scratches and scars when we were finished. ("Now look at that. Have you got any oil to put on it?" I told him I didn't think oil was good for a baseball. "Yes. That's right," he said. "Put dirt on it.")

He had gone to work early on Friday for some reason, had left before I went to breakfast. He came home on time, however. After supper I was standing by our front fence talking to a couple of classmates who were passing, when I heard him laughing. I looked up and saw the living room window that faced onto the porch was open. He was alone in there, for my mother was in the back yard again. The laughter was mad, like a child being tickled very hard, only the voice was the voice of a man, his voice.

"What's that?" one of my friends said.

The sound was so embarrassing I lied. I said, "The radio. I . . . I guess my father left it on." I drew away, started for the stairs. "I'll see you later . . . tomorrow," I said, and I ran up the stairs to investigate.

He wasn't there. Somewhere in the house, maybe in the basement, he was still laughing, saying things I

couldn't make sense of—"Let them put that one together."—laughing again, uproariously, no control at all.
I glanced down and saw the evening newspaper on his
footstool. I knew, I seemed to know, it had to do with
the paper, and I went over and scanned the front page
until I saw a headline that clamped itself onto my eyes
as if it had been crouching there, just waiting:

MYSTERY CALL
BAFFLES COPS

San Francisco. Police today tried to locate a
man who made a mysterious threatening phone
call shortly before eight this morning to Alden
Revere, President of Western and Pacific Sav-
ings and chairman of the recent "Gathering of
Tribes" ball sponsored by *The Loyal Sons and
Daughters of the Golden West.*

Revere said he was at home dressing for work
when he received the call: "I've never heard
anything quite like it," he said. "He (the caller)
had some sort of accent and told me plans were
underway to take measures against certain prom-
inent citizens in the city. He wasn't specific
about these measures, but, I, apparently was
first on his list."

Revere, who said he had had a few angry
phone calls in the past, "mostly from unhappy
customers who had not bothered to read the
terms of their loan contracts and tried to take
it out on us," added, "This was something altogether different."

He said the caller told him that the time had
come when he would either have to reform his
ways or suffer the consequences. "I was told to
do everything in my power to disband *The Loyal
Sons and Daughters* or I would not be around
to preside over next year's ball."

Police Detective Peter Ginella, assigned to
the investigation, said, "This has the smell of

one of those political things to me." He told
reporters there was little precedent for calls of
of this sort, "except for some of those Reds who
used to call the steamship officials during the
waterfront troubles of the Thirties but never
did anything." He seemed baffled, however, and
said, "It's pretty hard to come up with a motive.
Who would want to put an end to a charitable
organization like that?" He shook his head and
added, "Maybe it's not political, after all."

The investigation, Ginella said, would continue.

The paper fell from my hands. I turned, wanting to go
someplace, not knowing where to go. I ran through the
house. The door to the basement stairs was open. I
stopped and looked down, realizing the laughter had
stopped. I went on, raced to the kitchen, uneasy, wanting
to see my mother, not wanting to talk to her, just see her.
I began to feel queasy, almost having to throw up. I
looked out the window. I saw her. Then him. No laughter. He was tamely on his knees, a trowel in his hands,
following her along a strip of dirt she was furrowing for
seeds, him digging up loose weeds behind her, slinging
them over his shoulder toward the blackberry brush that
separated our yard from the neighbor's. In a moment I
saw his face; he was smiling. I stayed there watching. He
didn't miss a weed. Once he stopped, looked up, and let
out a single burst of laughter; it penetrated the window
before me. My mother looked around, startled. But then
he went on, keeping just a few feet behind her, finding
the weeds, getting rid of them. She went on too.

It seemed the natural place to go. I ran as far as the
bus depot, walked the rest of the way, saving my strength
for the climb. Just after I started zigzagging up the way
he had, I found the flattened box, the one I'd given him,
lying sideways on the grass where he had left it. I picked

it up, planning to take it to the top, where I would leave
it for someone else to use. I went on, crossing back and
forth across the hill, going up, until I stumbled on something and fell, having to catch myself with my free hand.
I turned back and saw that I had tripped over a large
stone; it was lying on the grass, where the grass had
been pressed down from the makeshift sleds passing over
it. I saw that it was the stone he had uprooted near the
top, the one he had kicked down the hill. I had been
sure the stone he had kicked had gone all the way to the
bottom; it had sounded as though it went to the bottom;
I moved closer and saw that it was the same stone, exactly
the same in size and shape. The makeshift sled, the one
I was carrying, had been lying just below the stone; he
had probably struck the stone, then tumbled off the sled.
He had left it on the grass. I knew it should be moved. It
was a danger to those who would slide down later. I
knew I should try to give it a heave and get it to the bottom. But I felt weak. I did not think I could raise it or
get it to the bottom. Maybe I would try to get it on my
way down. I left it where it was and continued toward
the top of the hill.

There was no wind, but the chilly air, circling down
from the top of the hill, felt like wind. The cold was
coming into the valley now and in the morning there
would be frost on the vacant lots and on the roof tops
and on the edges of walks, little splashes of it everywhere.
I had no jacket, only my t-shirt and suntans and I felt
the cold biting through them, into my skin and to my
bones. I moved faster to keep warm. By the time I made
it to the sitting stone I was shivering. I crouched forward,
clamping my arms together under my chest, and looked
out. The cold air seemed to have cleared the haze out of
the sky, for all the objects I looked at seemed sharp, vivid:
the tiny headlights far to the south, the street lamps, the
jagged outlines of the mountains to the west. Yet nothing
seemed to be moving; even the headlights, which I knew

were coming toward me, did not seem to be moving. Such a still and silent place. The cold had descended on it and frozen it and it would remain the same, the way it was, through the night; nothing would change until morning. I looked toward our neighborhood and tried to find our house. Sometimes I could spot it quickly; sometimes I couldn't. Now I couldn't locate it.

He would be talking. They would have come in from the yard and she would have put on the kettle for tea, or maybe he would have put it on because he did that sometimes after he drank—helped in the garden and made the tea—and he would be talking about everything except what had happened during the past week, about Uncle Dave dying and the price of groceries and the way old Berner was getting sourer by the day, every little detail on the surface of his life, down to the way the fumes smelled on the *Greyhound* bus he took to work, down to the price of a pig's tongue-and-cabbage lunch at Dinty Moore's across from the phone building, down to the twinge in that leg of his that came when he sat at his desk a certain way. And she would listen, nodding, for these were the things she understood about him, the things she could deal with.

Despite the cold I might have stayed there for a long time if it hadn't been for the lights. I glanced away and when I glanced back they blinked out. It had happened before when I was at home, but at home they went out gradually, a slow dimming of the lamp next to my bed, the room fading almost to darkness, then, just before reaching it, brightening again. This was different. Instantly I could see nothing. Because of high clouds there had been no stars and no moon and now, with the power off, everything in the valley suddenly was blotted out. In a moment everything about me seemed to have gone level, as though I were no longer on a hill at all but sitting someplace flat, surrounded by flatness. I looked around, searching for a reference point, but could see nothing. There was no connection between me and the town, the town and the hills, among any of us. It lasted only a few moments, but for those few moments everything around me seemed to have vanished. I was simply there, hanging in a void. Just as, in the distance, I noticed the pinpoints of a few car lights, just as I seemed about to get my bearings in the darkness, the lights came on, abruptly, just as they'd gone off. The experience frightened me, and I stood and started down the hill, quickly, not bothering to get a flattened box, sliding on my heels and the seat of my pants. Without the box I could control my speed and when I reached the stone he had shoved from the top I stopped and, crouching, bracing myself, tried to give it a strong push that would send it rolling past the fence posts. I couldn't get it up. Urgently, afraid the lights might go out again, I knelt and got my hands under its edges and with all my effort managed to raise the stone, getting it to its side. I turned it slightly and then, with much effort, gave it a push and sent it down, a crude wheel twisting blindly over lumps and pits, rolling, rolling, thumping in the darkness past the fence posts, surely getting past them this time, and stopping beyond them, where the hill went level. I followed it down, hurrying.

I entered the house quietly, and from the hallway I could hear him talking, talking and laughing; I listened. He was remembering something, an incident on their honeymoon: he had earlier promised her a ride in an airplane; neither of them had ever flown in an airplane; she said she would be frightened; he spent days trying to calm her; when they were married they went up—a Ford tri-motor, he recalled—and then, after all, it was he and not she who reacted: "A good joke on me, I must admit." He didn't elaborate. She was laughing, however, hard, in those unrestrained joyous bursts that made relatives laugh just listening to her. He had finished but she wanted to go on. When they were in their seats (more laughter), when they were in their seats, she remembered, he turned pale like a ghost and all wet with perspiration and then, when the steward came to tell them to buckle their belts, he looked up at the steward and his mouth opened but he couldn't speak, and the steward (great burst of laughter), the steward had to do it for him. I could hear him laughing too, appreciative hehs and hahs, nothing like her laughter: she was enjoying herself; he was being polite.

I went into the living room and found the newspaper beside the footstool, where I'd dropped it, and I took it and slipped out the front door and walked around to the backyard and put it in the incinerator. There were still embers glowing from cartons and papers one of them must have set off before coming inside. I watched the edges of the newspaper catch fire, then waited until the flames leaped up and I was sure the newspaper would burn through. I hurried through the basement and quietly up the center stairs and crept to my room, where they must have thought I'd been all the time.

I wanted to get to sleep before they finished talking, before he started for his room. I didn't. I had been in bed only a few minutes when I heard him come down the hall. He was tired now, walking unsteadily. It occurred to me that, with the hall light out, with him so unsteady, he might stumble on the edge of a rug and fall. I waited, listening, as if I was certain he would fall. Then he would call my mother or me to help him. I waited but he didn't fall. I heard him go into his room. The floor creaked as he changed into his pajamas and began to hang up his clothes. In the room he seemed to be moving sure-footedly. The bed sighed as he got into it. I knew there would be nothing thrown around; it would look so neat, the closet and the bedroom. I thought he might call her then, for something. But he didn't. There wasn't a sound and I knew he must be asleep or nearly asleep. I lay there silently for several minutes. My light was still on. I don't remember raising my leg out of the blanket but I do remember seeing it straighten against the wall, seeing my foot go—Smack!—against the wall.

"What's that?"

Smack! Smack!

"Mag! Is that you?"

Smack!

"Answer me!"

I could hear her coming and she appeared in the doorway and was looking in, helplessly looking in.

Smack!

"Do you hear me?" he shouted.

She turned in fright to the wall. I turned too. I had dented the plasterboard; I had dented it badly. "Jackie," she said in a shocked whisper, "what . . . what are you doing?" I was sorry, instantly sorry, knowing it would be she who would have to get it fixed, who would have to worry about getting it fixed.

"What's happening?" An insistent blast.

She stared at the wall, shaking her head. She did not seem angry, sad but not angry. "Stop it, Jackie," she said softly. "Please stop it."

"Maa-*aag!*"

When she backed out, her eyes were still on me, trusting me.

I thought she'd go to him. I was afraid she would go to him. She didn't and I was grateful. She went directly to the kitchen. I had an impulse to kick the wall once more. But I didn't.

"Come in here and tell me, I say!"

But she remained in the kitchen.

I could not get to sleep. When, after several curses, he went silent, I still could not get to sleep. I began to think about the stone. It was no obstacle to the sledders now but it would be a danger to someone walking in the darkness. Tomorrow, I thought, I would get something, a heavy piece of something—I didn't know what, steel maybe—and I would go up and strike at the stone, keeping striking at it until I had it broken into small pieces. Then I would take the pieces and hurl them into the trees so no one could trip on them or even feel them on their feet when they walked. Only after I planned what I would do about the stone could I get to sleep.

Matter of Ages

He is sitting cross-legged on the street corner watching the last of the fire. It is cold and he is sitting on his hands. He crossed the street with the others but could go no further. They said, "C'mon. You'd better hurry." He said, "I'm staying." They said, "You're crazy." He said, "Maybe, but I'm staying." They ran, shouting, "The cops will be here."

Now the cops are here. They are looking at the fire. They are shaking their heads. Above them the curtain is drawn over the big front window. After the fire started a little man with mournful baggy eyes appeared briefly from behind the curtain. With him was a little woman with tiny frightened eyes. Sitting on the corner he is thinking of those eyes and listening to the cops.
"Kids."
"Has to be."
"Must be foreigners upstairs."
"What else?"
They were in Jo-Jo's basement and Jo-Jo said, "Let's burn one on their lawn," and they did.

Now he is looking up, imagining the four eyes coming down at him through the fog. Sad eyes. Beaten eyes.

Dead eyes. The cops found him and took him to the station.

"What did you pull a stunt like that for?"
"Something to do."
"You know what a thing like that means to those people, huh?" He nodded. He knew what it meant, kind of, even in Jo-Jo's basement. He thought it was like putting a monster suit on and walking into a little kid's bedroom and waking him up. Maybe he is dreaming about a monster when you wake him up. Then he will really scream. He thought that's what it meant when they were walking up the hill from Jo-Jo's house.
"Then why, just tell me why?"
"Something to do."
"That's all?"
"It seemed like fun."

Jo-Jo read about them in the paper. All their lives wanting to come to the U.S.A. Living in prisons and concentration camps. Chased out of one country, then another. Saving pennies. Pennies stolen. Pennies lost. They still got to France. Years in France. Then they got to England. Years in England. Then Canada. Finally good old U.S.A. The papers made it a big story, Jo-Jo said, with their pictures and everything. The others listened. "You think they would put a story about your relatives or mine in the papers? Bet your ass they wouldn't." The others nodded. "Their kind run the paper," Jo-Jo said. "That's why. Their kind run everything."

They siphoned the gas out of Jo-Jo's father's pick-up and got matches at the grocery store.

"Why did you stick around?"
He didn't say. It still didn't make sense to him.

"He was sitting down, too."

"Why were you sitting?"

"And looking up at the fog. Crazy kid."

"What were you looking at?"

Eyes. That's what he was looking at. How could he say it? He couldn't.

"Answer."

"I can't."

"Call his parents."

His mother was an old lady, older than most of the mothers. His father was dead. His father had not liked them. She'd told him that. She was not crazy about them either. She said they stick together too much. One will always get another one a job, she said. Italians are the same, she said, only not as bad. She did buy once in a while at the delicatessen. But the one there, she said, is not like the other ones.

They took her into the room he was in. It had one little window at the top, with bars. One cop was holding her elbow. Her hair, white, was loose in the front and falling down to one side. She looked at him. She brushed back the loose hair with the back of her hand. "Why," she said, "why?"

The cop left and closed the door.

She went slowly to the wall and looked up at the window.

"Why?"

"We were in Jo-Jo's basement . . . ."

"Jo-Jo's basement," she repeated, spitting her words.

"I'm sorry, Mother."

"Sorry," she said dryly, wearily.

"I am. I was sorry as soon as I saw them looking." She turned to him. "Who looking?"

"The old people. Their eyes."

Her own eyes seemed to look at him out of boiling

water. She spoke hoarsely. "You were good and now you're no good."

A boy once called him one, and he got angry, maybe because his mother had just told him one of them had taken his father's supervisor job at the gas company or maybe because Mr. Walsh next door was saying they were starting to buy the good houses at the top of the neighborhood and pretty soon they'd be bringing their friends from Europe to live on their very block. It wasn't good to be called one.

He'd learned more in Jo-Jo's basement. It was like putting jigsaw pieces together, a couple of more pieces each time until you had a neat clear picture. The reason they were out to grab everything, your money and your house, is because it was part of Jo-Jo's people to be blind stubborn or Gino's to be winos and garbage men or Abner's to be dumb and lazy or his own to be hot-tempered. Only what was worse than grabbing everything someone had?

"Who else was with you?"

He shook his head.

"You want 'em laughing at you when you're in juvenile home?"

"I don't care."

"We'll pick 'em up sooner or later. We won't let 'em know. Save yourself trouble."

"I can't."

"You're stupid. You were stupid to stay on that corner but now you're really being stupid."

He'd been looking at the gray wall above the cop. He had to look away. He'd seen the eyes again. On the wall. They'd grown enormous.

"What's wrong?"

He put his hands over his face.

"You look sick."

He felt queasy, queasy and dizzy. He couldn't look at the wall.

"Talk and we'll take you out for a Coke and some doughnuts."

"I can't."

"Stupid, pal. You're really stupid."

When they left he didn't look up, but he saw the eyes in his mind for a while, and then the eyes faded and the two old people themselves came floating up in their place, the two of them without their eyes. Why were they such little people and why only the sockets, not the eyes? It should have been scarier than the eyes by themselves but it wasn't. It was as though he could go up to them and look into the holes. It was as though he should. It was as though they were standing there waiting for him to do that. He leaned forward, thinking that would bring him closer, but it didn't work. They receded as he moved. Then they disappeared with their black sockets. He opened his eyes. The eyes on the wall were gone. He felt different, relieved, at least that.

They caught Jo-Jo and the others. They brought them all to the door and let them look in.

"You dumb crapper," Jo-Jo said.

His mother returned.

"Father's coming down," she said. "He'll help."

"I don't want him."

"You'll do what he says." She was warning him. If he argued more she would have slapped him with the back of her hand. That was her way, slapping him and calling the priest. He went along, telling himself it was because she was old. The slaps didn't teach him anything. The priest he didn't like. He went along because he thought if he argued back too much she would get upset and maybe die. An old woman.

71

As she stood before him he pictured a dancing child, a little girl going around and around in circles in a short satin dress, spinning and spinning until she fell down giggling. He almost laughed at the thought, but didn't.

"He's the only one who can help you now," she said as she left the room. "You'll do what he says."

The priest came and spoke to him and he listened and nodded and the priest left and the cops came and one of them said, "You're lucky. We're letting you go."

He stood.

"Maybe you learned something from all this, huh?"

He walked past the cops to the door. He said nothing.

American Gothic

The events of that summer drift back slowly, darkly, like scenes from the dim gray movies we watched from the top of the highest balcony at the old Fox Theater on Market Street. We broke in through a side entrance late at night, crept past sleepy-eyed ushers clad like Marines in full dress, fled along the walls of the brightly lit stairways and landings, climbing upward, toward the darkness. Once, I recall, we arrived in time for the stage show, Duke Ellington and his band, playing again their hits of the late forties, but mostly we got there in time only for the feature film, or part of it. We took our seats and gazed down, hushed and myopic, as the theater darkened into a great bluish cavern, the smoky air flooded with music and the scenes of the film began to sweep relentlessly past us.

George was a little round foreigner, Greek or maybe Italian, and he had very bad eyes. We stole bottles of wine when he was in the lavatory in the back. Even if he heard us in the store, it took time for him to come up front, and then he couldn't see who it was until he got very close. We always got away.

It was Ditch's idea to steal. He was bigger, older and tougher than most of us. There were always boys like him around, in the neighborhoods or at high school or even working in libraries, where you might not expect them. You did what they said.

For some reason Ditch liked me. When I first arrived at the library, Ditch took the easy shelf (a wall of books at the west end of the reading room) away from Charlie and gave it to me. Charlie complained, saying he had been a page for two years and had earned the easy shelf. "Tough shit," said Ditch, who had been there longer than anyone and was head page. I thought he'd go on and give Charlie a reason—I was too new, too stupid for anything but the easy wall—but he didn't. Charlie shut up and took a hard section of shelves on the south wall: Fiction, R to Z.

On Saturday night, when it wasn't busy, all the pages met in the stacking room just behind the reading room desk. It was the best place to drink the wine. Miss Sweet worked the reading room desk on Saturday nights. She was a tall woman with a long bony face and sleepy eyes. She was very old, near retirement. She did not seem to notice us making noise.

Usually only the old men who in the daytime sat in the park across the street were in the reading room late at night. A lot of them if it was a cold night. The page who was on duty had to look under tables at closing time (11:00) because sometimes the old men lay down and slept there. At ten-forty-five Miss Sweet came into the stacking room and said, "Jackie, don't you think it's time to ask the gentlemen to leave?"

I always was careful to be polite to Miss Sweet because she was so old. "Yes, Miss Sweet," I said, "I'll do it right away."

"Thank you, Jackie." she said, and then she looked at us sitting slovenly on the tables beside the books piled for shelving on Monday morning. "Good night, boys," she said.

"Good night, Miss Sweet," most of us said, but someone, at Ditch's prodding, always added something like, "you old witch."

"Tsk, tsk, tsk," she said if she heard, which she usually didn't. "Whoever made that remark should be ashamed of himself."

"Are you ashamed of yourself, Charlie?" Ditch said.

"I am."

"Then apologize."

Charlie said, "I'm sorry, Miss Sweet."

"I'm surprised at you, Charles."

"I won't do it again, Miss Sweet."

When she closed the door, we laughed. Charlie, or whoever happened to make the remark, did not worry. He knew that Miss Sweet would never report him.

Once Ditch signaled me to say something funny to Miss Sweet, but I couldn't do it. When she left the room, he looked about and said, "One thing I hate is a guy with no sense of humor." But he didn't let them know he meant me. Later, when we went to the park in Civic Center after stealing the wine, he didn't speak to me, however, and I knew I'd failed him.

The others helped me get rid of the old men. There were always a few who lay across a pair of chairs or got under a table, and slept. When we finished with the ones who were seated, we wiggled the chairs of the sleepers, and kicked at the few that remained under the tables. I kicked them lightly on their butts, as most of the other pages did, but Ditch kicked hard. The old men groaned when Ditch kicked them and once one old man got sick and threw up.

We went to George's after work. George had long hours. From six in the morning to midnight. It was harder to steal wine late at night. He was always behind the counter then. Ditch sent one boy in by himself to buy a candy bar and start a conversation. Then another boy drifted in and stood behind the first boy so that George's vision was blocked by the first boy. The second boy backed up to the wine shelf across from the cash register and plucked off one or two bottles. He then nudged the first boy, who said good night to George and turned toward the door, giving the second boy time to go out ahead of him with the concealed wine. If George called to the second boy, "What you want?" he said, "I was just waiting for him (the first boy)." We had more wine.

I couldn't do the stealing. When I told that to Ditch I thought he'd jump all over me; he didn't. He said only that I had to do something and I'd better be willing to cover for someone else who could. I told him I didn't mind covering.

"You'd probably drop the bottle and break it anyway."

The others laughed.

"Guys that live with their mothers have no guts. You got to get tough, Jackie. My old man and I have a fist fight about every other day. How would you like that?"

I wouldn't, I told him.

I'd seen his father, who once came to the reading room, claiming Ditch had stolen some money from his drawer at home. The father drove a semi-truck for a paper company. He was about five-six but weighed (according to Ditch) two hundred pounds. It looked more like three hundred the night he came to raise hell with Ditch. He wore a tight black t-shirt his muscles were just about to rip to shreds. He told Ditch to give him back the money. Ditch said he didn't have it. The father put him up against the back wall of the stacking room and searched him. While the father slapped at his pockets and looked into his wallet, Ditch turned around and grinned and winked at the rest of us, who watched. When the father left the stacking room, Ditch called him a dumb runt. He said his old man picked on him because he was afraid someday Ditch was going to lay him out for good. "And I am," he said fiercely. "He'll think his truck ran over him."

If there was a good movie at the Fox on Market

Street, we went to the side and pried open an exit door. If there was something interesting at Civic Auditorium, like the annual boat show, we snuck through the delivery entrance at the back and saw it. Sometimes we went to one of the pool halls on Market Street and put our money together for a couple of games. One of us kept the bottle rolled up in his jacket. When anyone got thirsty, he took the jacket and went to the men's room.

Early in the morning (1:00) we all got on a streetcar, one that went through Twin Peaks tunnel. It was usually empty. When the car entered the tunnel, we started through it unscrewing light bulbs, or maybe we stood in back pulling the conductor's bell. The conductor complained, but Ditch or one of the older boys pushed him against the back window and cursed at him and said he was going to throw him off the car if he didn't shut up. He shut up. I enjoyed unscrewing the bulbs and didn't mind pulling the rope on the bell, except when the conductor started to complain. When I pulled pranks Ditch stood back and laughed, delighted. Much of my pleasure came from making him laugh. When the motorman sensed the lights going off, he sped up. The car went so fast it zigzagged from side to side. One of the older boys climbed out on the raised cowcatcher in back and went the rest of the way in the open air, screaming like Tarzan. If there were other riders, we cursed at them and did crazy things like offer them wine. The streetcar had to slow down for a turn at the end of the tunnel. That's when we jumped off. There was a workman's ladder before the car reached the end of the approachway, where there might be police cars.

We were usually out of wine by then. For a while we stood under a telephone pole and listened to someone tell dirty stories. Finally we split up and walked home in little groups, singing and throwing rocks at street lights.

Then the library hired a new page. The biggest differ-

ence we noticed between him and us was not his color—
we all knew a few black kids at school—but that he
carried a knife, a long, thin pocket knife. When I say the
biggest difference we noticed I mean the biggest difference Ditch noticed because if Ditch didn't notice something you noticed you figured it wasn't worth noticing,
and you stopped noticing it.

We were in the stacking room getting louder and
louder one Saturday night when Abner pulled out the
knife. Abner had hardly spoken the first couple of days
he worked there. He sorted his books and put them on
the reading room shelves and went to whomever was
working at the desk and asked was there anything else
he could do, and if there wasn't he went to a corner of
the stacking room and read a magazine that looked like
Life but had blacks on the cover.

We were drinking when Ditch looked up and saw the
knife. Abner was working on his fingernails.

"What you got that for?" he asked.

Abner wasn't drinking with us. He looked up with his
big frog eyes. "What?" he said.

"The knife," Ditch snapped. "Why do you need a big
pocket knife to fix your nails?"

Abner looked at the knife and then at Ditch. He
didn't answer. Aside from Ditch he was the strongest
looking boy in the room.

"Hey," said Ditch, getting off his chair. "You hear
what I said?"

"I heard," said Abner, who was looking at the magazine again.

"Well?"

Abner looked up slowly, right at Ditch. "I don't
know."

"Gimme that," said Ditch.

Abner held the knife in his right hand. It was still
open. The tip of the blade was pointed toward Ditch's
middle.

"You hear?" said Ditch.

Abner didn't move.

Just then Miss Sweet opened the door and said, "Jackie, don't you think it's time to ask the gentlemen to leave?"

"Yes, Miss Sweet. I'll do it in . . . a few minutes."

"Hurry now," she said, standing at the door. "It's getting late." She wasn't looking at Abner's knife. She probably wouldn't have seen it if she had been.

I couldn't move, too interested to see what would happen between Ditch and Abner when the door closed. No one made fun of her that night. We were all waiting.

But Abner raised his head. Slowly he closed the magazine and then the knife. He stood up and slid the knife into his pocket. He did not look at Ditch as he walked past him to the door.

He had cooled things off, but you would have had to be stupid blind not to know that sooner or later Ditch would go at Abner or Abner at Ditch. Sometimes one or two of us went home early, but that night everyone tagged along.

In the vacant lot beside George's store, Ditch said, "Abner's first night with us. I think Abner ought to steal the wine." No one had asked Abner to come along, but he had. "How about it, Abner?" he said. It was dark there in the lot. Looking, you could not see Ditch's sneer, but you could hear it in his voice.

Abner's big eyes, intense and curious, were shining in the light of a distant street lamp. "Explain the stealing," he grunted. He sounded a little scared now.

Someone told him how it was done, and then Ditch said to Abner, "Okay, you buy the candy bar, and I'll get the wine."

But someone said, "He can't go. George won't let Negroes in his store."

"That's right," said Ditch. He looked at Abner.

79

"You're lucky you're a Nig." He came down hard on
the "Nig."

He waited for Abner to jump at the word. But he
didn't.

Ditch stole the bottle while Charlie covered.

When we got to the pool hall, Abner said good night.

"Where you goin'?" Ditch said.

"I don't know how to play, man."

"You're gonna learn, man," Ditch said. He arrogantly
broke between a couple of us, grabbed Abner's shirt and
pulled him up the pool hall stairs. Abner didn't resist
at all. I was surprised, certain by now that Ditch was
afraid of nothing. He reminded me of an oversized
Jimmy Cagney the way he swaggered; in fact, he sort
of looked like Jimmy Cagney in the face. "C'mon, Nig,"
he said, heading for a corner table. The rest of us
followed.

Ditch took a table only for himself and Abner. For
nearly two hours he tried to show Abner how to play.
Every few minutes he called him stupid and grabbed the
stick away from him and bent down to show him what
he was doing wrong.

Finally we all stood and watched, waiting for Abner
to blow up, sure he would. But he didn't.

When it was over, Ditch slapped him on the back and
said, "What you think of this game?"

Abner, despite the abuse Ditch had given him,
shrugged and said, "Ain't bad."

There were looks of disappointment all around. A ter-
rific fight hadn't come off. I was relieved, sure one of
them would have ended up in the hospital. Knowing
Ditch, however, I didn't think he was finished with Abner
yet. Neither did the others, I guess. Everyone tagged
along when we started up Market toward the tunnel
entrance. Every once in a while Ditch would duck into
an unlighted store doorway and the rest of us would
follow. There we'd drink some wine. Abner drank too,

slowly at first, making horrible faces. But then he stopped making faces and drank faster.

For a while Ditch seemed pretty friendly to him, but then he started saying things about Abner's toughness. "He's not a bad pool player now, but how does he go in a fight? That's what I'd like to know." When he spoke, he addressed everyone but Abner.

Abner knew how to handle it. He played deaf.

But then Ditch got onto the knife again. "Why does he carry that thing anyway? Can't he fight like the rest of us? I've heard about these Pachukes and Niggers."

Finally, fearing the worst, frightened, I said, "Why don't you lay off, Ditch? Abner isn't bothering anyone."

"The hell he ain't. That knife of his bothers me."

"What's wrong with a knife?" someone said.

"I didn't say anything was," said Ditch. "I just want to know."

Someone added, "My old man says the streets are getting so full of punks everyone is going to have to carry a gun or a knife pretty soon."

"Your old man is chicken shit," said Ditch, giving the boy a sidelong look. He turned back to Abner. "How about it Abner? How come you carry a knife?"

We were nearing a doorway. Abner stopped and looked up, fixing his eyes, now nearly closed from the wine, on a dark building across the street. "Man," he said thoughtfully, in a kind of light-hearted squeal, "I don't know. I just don't know."

Abner's tone seemed to anger Ditch. "The hell you don't," he said, facing Abner, his clenched fists on his hips.

Now Abner looked patiently up at a trolley wire.

"How long you been carrying it?"

Abner looked at him coldly, "Don't know."

"Where you from?" someone said.

"Alabama," he said.

"You didn't carry a knife there?" Ditch said.

"No."

"No wonder Niggers come to San Francisco," said Ditch to everyone but Abner. "It's the only place they're allowed to carry knives. Niggers and queers and foreigners and old people. All the outcasts come to San Francisco."

Abner's eyes were back on the trolley wire. Finally he let out a noisy sigh. He shook his head. "I carry it because I carry it. I guess that's about all I can say."

"Well, that ain't a reason," Ditch growled. "How 'bout you givin' it to me to carry?"

"Uh uh," said Abner, putting his hand on his pocket. "Can't do that."

"Otherwise I just might have to take it."

Abner backed out of the doorway we had entered. "You just come on then if you have to, I ain't giving it up by myself."

Ditch could not seem to decide whether or not to move after Abner. He crouched down, glared at him, and then straightened. He stuck out his forefinger and said, "God damn you, Nig. You're gonna gimme that before the night's over."

" 'Fraid I can't, Ditch," Abner said politely.

"Streetcar'll be here in a minute," someone said. "Let's have a drink." We hurried to the tunnel streetcar stop and drank.

The conductor, also black, watched us suspiciously as we got on. The streetcar was nearly empty. We went peacefully to the center of the car and sat down.

Ditch explained our operations to Abner. As he listened, he seemed uneasy. Now and then he looked back at the conductor. "What do you do this for?" he said.

"To pass the time," said Ditch. "But tonight we're gonna just sit here and watch you. You're gonna do all the work. You got yourself a real daddy back there. You give him some real fun. And if you don't, we're gonna take away that knife, and I'm gonna personally beat shit out of you." He was sitting very close to Abner. Several of his closest followers were leaning over them.

I had been trembling since the conversation in the doorway. I knew whose side I'd be on if a fight started. Not Ditch's. That made me even more nervous. I said from across the aisle, "Ditch, why don't you leave him alone?"

"Shut up," Ditch said. "You're still a baby. When you turn into a man, you give me advice."

Abner was clearly frightened. He sat very still, staring straight ahead. Then he rose slowly and walked back to the conductor. The conductor kept his eyes warily on him. Because of the loud noise of the streetcar echoing through the tunnel, you could not hear what Abner was saying.

"Quit starin'," Ditch said.

We turned around and faced the front, waiting to hear bells ringing or glass breaking. Nothing happened for a long time, and then there was a yell. We looked back but could see neither Abner nor the conductor. Ditch was the first to leap out of his seat and race back.

We found them on the floor. The old conductor's mouth was bleeding. Abner was sitting on top of him, about to bring his big fist down once more. Ditch grabbed his fist. Then he held his free hand to keep the rest of us away. He seemed to want to be sure of some- thing before he really stopped Abner. Every time Abner broke free and struck, we all, even Ditch, flinched. Finally Ditch pulled Abner off the conductor. The beaten old man lay there and looked fiercely up at Abner. He muttered one word: "Traitor!" Abner was grunting like a chained and angry dog, fighting to get back at him. The streetcar began to slow down. Ditch pulled Abner away, and we moved quickly to the open step.

There was some wine left. We killed it in silence in

an unfinished house on a hill several blocks from the tunnel entrance. Sitting around a dusty future bedroom, we could see through the window the tops of many houses. All the roofs were coated in blue moonlight. The new neighborhood was like those most of us lived in. The house, the bedroom itself, was identical to many of ours.

Abner was alone in a corner, still panting heavily. He had said nothing from the time we left the streetcar.

"Hey, Ab," someone called, "how did it start?"

Abner stopped panting. He hesitated, then said, "He made me an insult."

"Huh?" said Ditch.

Facing Ditch, speaking in a low voice that made me think it had to be either that or shouting, he told us he had gone to the back of the streetcar, not intending to play with the bell, not intending to do anything, just to stand there with the conductor, then get off at the end of the tunnel and leave us. He looked across at Ditch, hesitated, then said, "If you would have come back there, man, I wouldn't have let you do anything. Know that?"

Ditch said, "Bullshit," and started to stir as if he were going to get up and go across the room. He didn't, too interested, as all of us were, in what Abner was going to say next.

"First thing is he calls me a minstrel boy. He says, 'You got your face painted up, just for the show, didn't you, boy?' I asks him what he means by that. He says my face was painted. Underneath it I was white just like those others, meaning yours. He says go ahead and steal my money 'cause that's what those white boys do. I start to tell him I'm not going to do anything but he don't listen and says I'm a little field slave and lots of things and I tell him shut up but he don't and then he calls me a traitor to my own race and that's when I hit him." Abner stood up now, had walked over to the window and was looking out. "You can't make me one. He can't. Nobody can. What'd he have to say that for?"

"It don't matter," said Ditch.

"I ain't a traitor. He shouldn't of said that."

"That's right. That's right," said Ditch, wanting to get on to something else.

Abner turned abruptly. "I hate you, man." He was looking squarely at Ditch. He shook his head and turned back to the window. He reached into his pocket and slowly removed his knife.

Ditch, on the floor, started squirming back, fussing with his jacket as he moved.

I thought this was going to be the fight we'd all hung around for. But Abner, with a flip of his hand, tossed the knife out the window. He turned back, again to Ditch. "I ain't afraid of you," he said. "I hate you but I ain't afraid."

"Hey!" Charlie, against the wall was pointing. "What's that?"

I turned.

Something was glistening in front of Ditch. In the dim light I could see him moving it back, to the side, toward his jacket pocket.

"It's a . . . it's a gun," said Charlie, who was closest to Ditch.

The gun was back in Ditch's pocket. He had taken it out when Abner had shown the knife, but now it was back, secure in his pocket.

I was stunned the moment Charlie had said "gun." Ditch was liable to do nearly anything, but a gun . . . . That seemed to turn all else inside out. I juggled with the recognition, not knowing what to do with it.

Charlie seemed to speak for all of us: "You never told us about that, Ditch."

"Whyn't you mind your own god damn business?"

"But . . . ."

"What the hell you think I did with the dough I stole from my old man, buy candy bars?"

"Jesus," Charlie said. "Jesus Christ!"

Abner hadn't moved.

"Whyn't you sit down?" Ditch said to him, making it a command, not a request.

"Don't want to."

"You better," Charlie said. He turned to Ditch, then back to Abner, finding in the passage of his eyes a new knowledge that had to be communicated. He had known Ditch longer than any of us and seemed certain when he said, "He'll use it."

"I ain't sitting down," Abner said.

"Sit!"

"Jesus," Charlie whispered.

Ditch's hand glided back, as if responding to the pull of an invisible rope.

Someone made a whimpering noise.

"Please don't take it out again, Ditch," I said.

He didn't seem to hear. Or maybe the attention he was getting urged him to go through with it. He removed the pistol, very small, held it in front of his stomach, pointed at Abner's stomach, raised his left hand to the weapon, and made the hammer click back.

Charlie had come a certain distance and could seem to go no farther: "Jesus."

Abner had backed all the way up against the window, eyes wide, a pair of brightly burning lights fixed on the pistol.

"Sit down," Ditch said.

He didn't move.

I stood shakily.

"Sit down." This time it was for me.

"Ditch," I said weakly.

"Sit down."

But something drew me forward. While I sensed the danger, I was not acting to challenge it; I was just moving, the way Ditch's hand had moved toward the gun, as if that was the thing I, my rope, was causing me to do next. I saw something moving on the other side of the room. One of the others. Also moving toward Abner. Charlie. He was coming in slow mechanical steps, approaching from the other side.

"Everybody sit down!"

In a moment Charlie was next to me, in front of Abner, facing Ditch.

"What the hell you two doin'?"

"Put . . . put it back in your pocket," Charlie said.

"Yeah, Ditch," someone said from behind him.

"Why should I put it back?" Ditch said in a new uncertain voice. "If he had a knife, why can't I have this?"

"You got to put it back, that's all," Charlie said, trying to sound calm.

"Got to, huh?"

"You just got to," Charlie said. "You just got to, Ditch."

My legs quivered. They seemed about to give way. I could feel Charlie's arm next to mine. I wasn't facing Ditch defiantly, I was just standing there, before him, in front of Abner, beside Charlie, waiting for something that had started finally to stop, as if it was bound to stop, the way a downpour of rain that interrupts a game on the street has to stop.

"You . . . you might shoot *me* . . . or *Jackie*." Charlie had been searching and now he'd found what he wanted. "That's why, Ditch."

In a moment there was a click, hammer forward, and the gun went down to his side. "That's a good enough reason," he said, seeming relieved. "Yeah."

When the gun was back in Ditch's pocket, Abner stepped forward, opening a space between Charlie and me. He took a few steps toward Ditch, then turned and moved to the door. Quickly he was gone. The room went silent. Then someone got up in back and went out, fol-

lowing Abner. Then someone else. Before I realized what
was happening, Charlie left me and went out. The door
was open now. Abner had closed it behind him, but the
second person to leave had left it open, and it was still
open and, one by one, everyone was leaving. Finally
there were only Ditch and me.

"Pricks." Ditch was still seated. He mumbled the
words into the floor: "Nigger lovin' pricks."

I stood there, not knowing what to say to him, then—
it seemed the only choice I had—I left the room too.

"You're one of them too, you baby!" he yelled after
me. "The only reason I didn't shoot you is 'cause you're
such a god damn baby!" He kept shouting but I couldn't
make out what else he said.

The others were walking ahead of me, in a line, all
walking separately, twenty, thirty, forty yards apart,
about six altogether. I felt strong walking behind them.
I thought Ditch might be coming along behind me; that
frightened me, but I didn't look back; I kept myself from
looking back. I wanted to keep feeling strong. Way up
in front was Abner. When he approached the corner
where you turned toward the streetcar stop, a street light
from behind shone on him in a way that momentarily
made him seem white; someone else. But by the time he
reached the corner the harsh light went off him and he
was himself again. One by one they went around the
corner. I was the last one around.

At the car stop we talked about what happened. Someone said Charlie and I had more guts than the whole god
damn U.S. Army. Charlie denied it. He said it would
have taken more guts for him to pick up someone else's
bloodied body which is what he would have had to do
if Ditch had pulled the trigger on Abner. I hadn't thought
of that, but it made sense. Anything might have made
sense. I still didn't know why I'd done what I'd done.
Finally someone asked Abner, who had thanked Charlie

and me about twenty-five times already, if he was going
to stick it out at the library.

"Why not?" he said.

It took a while for his answer to sink in but then there
were nods all around. Of course. Why not? Why not for
any of us.

Ditch never did arrive at the car stop. Funny, but no
one looked toward the corner to see if he'd come around.
No one seemed to care. I guess if he had come around
and tried something, with or without gun, none of us
would have backed off, unless maybe he'd gone crazy
and come around shooting.

On Monday Charlie arrived at work a little late. He
told us he'd run into Ditch in a soda fountain on Mission
Street. Ditch, he said, was quitting the library. "He told
me his old man was getting him a job on the trucks, rid-
ing as back-up driver for the old man himself."

I thought someone would laugh at the reason as
phony. No one did. Maybe it *was* the true reason. Ditch
had recently turned eighteen, was old enough to get a
chauffeur's license. I pictured him in the truck cab beside
his father, fingering the pistol in his pocket. Firecrackers,
I thought, if they ever got into an argument.

Charlie also said Ditch had had a message for Abner.
Charlie delivered it straight-faced. "He said he'd meet
you any time or any place. No weapons. Just bare fists.
You just name it." Charlie kept his laughter inside until
he finished. Then he broke up, slapping his hand hard
on the top of a stack of books. Abner was grinning, just
shaking his head and grinning.

Later someone cut a picture of a cooked chicken out
of *Family Circle* magazine and stuck it on the wall above
where Ditch used to sit. In red crayon across the chicken
was Ditch's name. For days there were a lot of jokes and
insults about Ditch.

One day, when we were all laughing, Abner stopped

and looked at the chair at the end of the stacking room. It was the only chair in the room, the one from which Ditch had tossed his orders, the one from which he'd challenged Abner. Abner kept looking at the chair, finally turning away with a fearful gaze. "That white-ass son-of-a-bitch nearly killed me," he said as if he just now became aware of the fact. His remark was good for more laughs, but also for a subsequent silence in which we all, I think, started to weigh what had nearly happened.

There weren't many jokes after that. Now and then I'd get puffed up and think it had been like a no-bull western movie, and I'd size myself up with the latest cowboy actor who'd hooked me with wondrous moves. But most of the time, often when I was alone in the stacking room, I'd look at Ditch's chair or some other object that reminded me of him and feel a low chill, testicles turning to ice cubes, remembering. At such times I'd get out, maybe go stack some books or head for the reference room and get a drink of water.

It occurred to me once that Ditch might have been right in what he'd said about me being a baby, even that night in the house, especially that night. I remembered the way infants crawled out on ledges or into the paths of cars if you let them. Maybe I'd done something like that. I hoped, was pretty sure in fact, that it had been more than that. I never did know for certain and finally just stopped worrying about it.

Funeral

When he was a young man in college he had this idea: he would write a story of his own funeral. The teacher said, "You can't do that. How can you write about what you haven't seen?"

He didn't write the story.

They were winding up the hill with this mahogany box and he saw them in his dreams but not only in his dreams. They put the box in a hole. His mother was there.

He worked in the city after his classes, downtown in the city, and there was a man with no legs who sat on a coaster selling pencils. The man's clothes were dirty and he had one eye.

"Do you ever have thoughts you're afraid to share?"

"Not often," his friend said.

Somewhere he read that Sartre, though afraid, felt freer in Nazi-occupied Paris than he had anywhere else. Sartre said every move he made had significance. Sartre said he knew then what freedom was.

He told that to a teacher.

The teacher said, "Well, that makes sense."

Philip F. O'Connor

Someone banged it against the side of the grave and it tipped and fell and everyone heard it crack but no one suggested raising it up again and repairing the box. Not even his mother.

"I've hardly seen a funeral, maybe one or two, but I dream about my own all the time," he told his friend.

The friend said, "You can't take such things too seriously."

He said, "Do you ever dream such things?"

The friend said, "No."

There was this girl who lived next door when he was a child and her father beat her often and she went into the back yard and cried but when she came out to the street to play she was never crying. She did well in school and was now a chemical technician, living at home still.

"It's amazing the things you see that aren't in books," he told his friend.

His friend agreed.

His friend became an accountant after graduation. He himself drove a truck. He would drive the truck until he could decide what to do.

"You should make yourself some money," his friend said.

"I'm not very ambitious."

"And meet people. Who can you meet driving a truck?"

"No one really."

He lived by the sea. The ships came in, the ships went out. When the work was light he drove to the park near the bay. The water was mysterious and so were the ships, especially the ones going out. He watched them for hours. Where were they going?

A leg came out of the coffin, naked, white, wiggling. There was no sound. Just the leg.

The truck was an old truck and went slowly up hills. The city had many hills. There was something between him and the truck, a kind of trust. You could leave the truck in gear on some hills. On others you had to put on the brake. He got to know the truck and the hills where the truck would stay and the hills where it would not. There was no reward for knowing the truck and the hills. The man who owned the business died. His son sold the business and the truck.

He sought another job, on trucks. There was something about being able to think and speculate and wonder while sitting behind a wheel. Trucks were the best for him. He would drive another truck. A big truck on highways.

One employer said, "Experience is important if you want to drive one of those rigs. You haven't enough experience."

Another said, "Are you in the union?"

He wasn't.

He took up, finally, with a drug store, driving a small truck for a chain of drug stores. The driving was constant.

In the evenings he went to the library to find books on the mind that dealt with questions he couldn't answer. It was hard for him to find the books he wanted. Once in a while a phrase suggested something: "We live the dreams of ancestors as well as of ourselves." But, really, very little.

A man reached in and plucked off the leg. They marched down the hill and put it in a fire. After the fire they put the ashes in a wheelbarrow and took them up the hill. They sprinkled them on top of the dirty coffin. They filled in the hole. The mother hadn't cried but when the dirt was on the coffin her knees buckled and she cried. They pounded the dirt with their feet. They sprinkled seed on the dirt. They put up no headstone. The grass grew. You could not tell someone was buried there.

He got deliveries done early one day and had some time for the bay. He was sitting on the strip of sand by the water when two girls came by. They were high school girls. They sat not far from him. They did not look at him. He threw little stones into the water where it lapped. He listened:

"He's so kooky."

"I know. I know. Geraldine dated him and said he took his shoes off at the movie."

"No!"

"Honest to God!"

"Then he wanted to take her for chili dogs out near the beach. You know, at the amusement park."

"That filthy place?"

"She said she wouldn't go. He took her home and asked her to go fishing with him the next day."

"Fishing?"

"She said she had a surfing date with Eddie."

"Oh god!" Laughter. "Fishing!"

"Imagine!"

He was lying down now and his arms were over his head, flat against the sand and his face was in the sand and he tasted the salty taste of the sand and clip-clapping of the little waves went on and went on and he listened and tasted the salt taste of the sand and fell asleep.

When he got up he was cold. He took his truck back and was reprimanded for being late. He understood the reprimand. As he headed for the streetcar he saw a manhole cover pulled partly away from its hole. Had he not been looking he might have missed it and fallen in, all the way in or partly in. But he saw it and avoided it.

A San Francisco Woman

Joe, a bear of a man, thundered up the stairs, banged open the front door, making the two old chimes sound in trembling response, and shouted, "Where the hell's the car?"

Sheila, whose recent flabbiness betrayed every one of her unkempt thirty-seven years, had just stooped to open the drawer of the only appliance in the house which worked consistently, the stove. She paused, listened, then calmly opened the drawer and removed a frying pan. She rose wearily and turned toward the noise with a groan only she could hear.

Francis, their son, had taken the eight-year-old *Pontiac* to a high school football game. Joe had warned him to have the car home by six o'clock. It was now a little after five-thirty.

"C'mon, Clarence," he said loudly as he thumped toward the kitchen.

It was Friday, Joe had begun his weekly binge. The pattern each week was the same: five days of tension, two of release. He had started drinking at the brewery this afternoon. Now, home a little early, he wanted the car for his first trip to Malone's, a tavern just outside the city limits. There he would stay, except for a few trips home to eat and sleep and, most of all she was sure, to bully her and Francis. Late Sunday evening he would come home for the last time. By Monday morning, he would be sober, and the pattern would begin again. Maybe he would hurriedly stuff some food into his belly before he left; maybe he wouldn't. She didn't care. Once she had cared. Once she had told herself, I'll stand up to him, but the resolution, like herself, had acquired a certain flabbiness. Except for a rare reply, usually angry and always futile, she sat back and took it. She would go ahead and cook supper, trying to ignore him.

"In here." He had rumbled to the kitchen and was now searching the bottom of the broom closet for the half-full bottle of *Early Times* he had left there last Sunday night. He found it, plucked off the cork and took a drink. He pushed past her and got two glasses from the cupboard above the stove.

A tiny man came reeling into the kitchen. He had stupid sleepy eyes like Stan Laurel in the old movie comedies. His body seemed no thicker than one of Joe's legs. He was no taller than Joe's chin. Joe was five feet and eleven inches.

"Take these to the living room."

Clarence took the glasses and bowed two or three times to Sheila as, backwards, he followed Joe toward the hall. At the doorway he turned and wagged his head, giving Sheila a little smile.

"Be a nice day tomorrow if it clears up."

She nodded, smiling back at him.

"You never know though." He started to turn, stopped, looked at the glasses in his hand, then at her. He raised one of the glasses toward her. "How about you?"

She shook her head.

"Oh, well." He shrugged and turned, going into the hall.

"Nice wife you got there," he said to Joe in the living room.

"The hell she is. Here. Give me those glasses."

Sheila crossed the room and looked out the little win-

dow facing the gray wall of the house next door. Dark
fists of fog swept down, into the open stair well. The fog
had hung heavily over the neighborhood all morning.
In the afternoon it had thinned to a bright haze. Now,
swiftly, it was returning.

All of the houses in the neighborhood were set side
by side, no space between, except for the stair wells, small
light wells, an occasional indoor patio. As in most
houses, the stairs here led to the basement-garage beneath
the house. She saw the garage in her mind's eye, stuffed
with junk, the accumulation of nineteen years of marriage
—Francis's old bike with the front wheel mangled, the
graying floor of the unfinished room at the back that Joe
had started to build twelve years ago, an enormous dusty
trunk containing her dead mother's clothes and memen-
tos, the broken parts of a double bed, a rusting baby car-
riage, other bits and pieces that now and then would fall
to the floor, surprising her, when she was down there
searching for something. Though Joe moaned about having to keep the *Pontiac* on the street and Francis constantly complained that he couldn't find a mitt or a ball
or something, she no longer tried to straighten up the
garage. "Why don't you help?" she said when they began
to gripe. "I can't do it all myself." That usually shut
them up, at least for a while. One of these days, she often
promised herself, she'd call the *St. Vincent de Paul* and
have them back a truck up at the door and take everything out.

She turned, hearing Joe's small talk, derisive and
mocking: " 'So, look,' I tell him, 'if the stuff's coming
through and the gauge still reads zero, you know god
damn well there's something wrong with the gauge.
That's the thing that's got to be off. Right?' I mean anyone with half-a-brain could figure it out. Hah. Not him.
Not him."

Unlike Joe's other friends, this Clarence wasn't arguing with him. Joe liked someone to give him an argu-

97

ment, someone who was like a baseball bat whacking back, Joe throwing harder and harder until he began to get the balls by, which sooner or later he did. That she didn't understand. What fun could it be arguing with Joe? What fun when you knew you'd never win? Better to take all the pitches. Or not even be there to take any. Or do something else, like this Clarence. He was no bat. He was letting Joe finish, then calmly replying:

"You got to figure, Joe, these guys never learned anything about pressures and valves in the first place."

"Damn right they didn't."

"They don't know what they're talking about, that's for sure, but then you got to figure somebody put them on the job. I mean the one who puts them on the job, he should know better."

"None of 'em know a god damn thing, the supervisors least of all."

"That's just what I'm driving at, Joe. It starts at the top. You can't blame the shift foreman when someone sticks him there when he shouldn't. See what I mean?"

"Yeah. Yeah. I see."

"That's all I'm saying."

"Yeah . . . yeah." Gurgle gurgle. There was silence, unusual, then Joe, stung by a new thought, said, "I'll tell you what they ought to do about those god damn supervisors."

She went to the stove, where she had laid out slices of sole. She put them on the pan, making sure to lay them down so the edges didn't overlap. *Nice wife,* she remembered as she sprinkled salt on top of the fish. And then: *The hell she is.* She put down the big shaker and raised her eyes to the clock above the stove, studying it, as if the rest of the conversation, the things they hadn't said about her, might be emblazoned on its face. Behind her she heard their voices, but she didn't listen to what they were saying, for her memory, as it did so often lately, had begun to descend on old events, stirring like a stick in cold ashes.

"Do you want to go or don't you?"
"I want to go but I don't want to cause any . . . ."
"He'll be happy to take you."
"Are you sure?"
"I'm sure. You can't miss the Invitational. It's not like any other dance. You *have* to . . . . Listen. If you don't want to call him, I'll do it for you."
"Ellen . . . ."
"Do you want me to?"
She hesitated, then nodded.
George called her later, sometime after school. He was going to have to make it short, he said, because of foot-ball practice, but he said Ellen had called him at school and sure, it would be great to take her. There were a lot of other guys going from St. Ignatius. "I won't get bored," he said. "No kidding."
That evening mother altered the gown Sheila's cousin had worn to the dance two years earlier. Frankie pranced around her, watching her stand very still in front of the long mirror in their parents' bedroom. Her mother pinned up the hem and said worrisome things about the top being too low:
"I don't think Sister Imelda will like it at all."
"Gerrie wore it that way."
"It was pinned together. I remember."
"Times have changed, Mother."
"Two years isn't two decades. I can just imagine what Sister will say."
Sheila laughed and said, "Oh, Mother, you sound so *old.*"
Later, at supper, they all chatted about the dance. Her father promised to go down to that Italian florist on Geary Street the next morning and get her a big geranium

for the front of the dress. Sheila laughed at that, knowing
he was serious, knowing he thought a big geranium
would look pretty on the dress. Her mother kept her in
front of the big mirror at the end of the hall until after
midnight on Friday, making last-minute adjustments.

She got up late on Saturday morning. She was eating
breakfast when George called. He said he had caught a
bad case of the flu and wouldn't be able to take her. "I'm
sorry, Sheila." He went on, telling her how it hit him
just after football practice the afternoon before, saying
it was lousy the way things like this happened, saying he
had tried to think of someone to take his place but
hadn't been able to. "Don't worry about it," he said.
There was a long pause. Finally she thanked him for
calling, said she hoped he'd feel better soon, then lowered the phone slowly to its cradle and went to her room.
It was at least an hour before she found the strength to
tell her parents.

That night, to get her mind off the dance, she took
Frankie to a movie on Geary Street. The movie, about
pirates, bored her but she enjoyed watching Frankie, on
the front of his seat, turning every now and then ("Geez,
Sheila, did you see that guy fall off the sails?"), turning
back, waiting for the next sword fight. Afterwards they
walked to Foster's Cafeteria several blocks down Geary,
where she'd promised to buy him some hot chocolate.
When she pushed open the door, holding it for Frankie,
she looked up and saw George in a back booth. He was
with some of his St. Ignatius friends, football players in
their bright red jackets with big S.I.'s on the chests. He
wasn't sick, did not look sick at all. They were all laughing. For an instant she thought they'd all seen her, and for
some reason were laughing at her. But they hadn't seen;
none of them were even looking at her. Quickly she
grabbed Frankie by the hand and pulled him back, onto
the sidewalk. She tugged him, whining, over to Clement
Street, to a diner with only six or seven chairs, no other

customers but themselves. The man behind the counter said he had no hot chocolate so she bought Frankie a *Coke*. On the way home he complained: "I wanted hot chocolate. That's what you promised me, Sheila." She ignored him.

In her bedroom later she listened to Anson Weeks music on the radio from the Fairmont Hotel, waiting for the sad ballads, sure she would feel the hurt when they came on. But she didn't feel it. There was no hurt at all, no surprise. She lay on the bed and remembered her mother's maxims about the deeper qualities that made for friendships and courtships and marriages that lasted and *meant* something. She also thought of the picnics on Sundays, salves against the lonely nights. They'd go, six or seven girls, in one of the family cars, to McNear's Beach or Stinson Beach or Half Moon Bay, out of the cold wet city, into the soothing sunlight. There was a picnic planned for the day after the Invitational Ball.

Ellen drove her father's car. On the way to McNear's she said she and George had had a terrible fight when she got home from the dance. Sheila guessed what it had been about and hoped Ellen wouldn't tell the others, who possibly didn't know what George had done. Ellen didn't tell, pal that she was, said just enough to let Sheila know she hadn't put up with the dirty trick her brother had pulled. Her own brother, she said, and he disgusted her. Winding through the Marin hills Sheila listened to reports of the dance and the parties afterwards:

"You should have seen Dave after someone put whiskey in his *Coke!*"

"I'll bet he was funny."

"Funny? Oh, Sheila! He got in the middle of the floor and said he was going to take all his clothes off!"

"No!"

"Peggy said she'd go home without him if he did. So he didn't."

It had been fun and she would have loved being there,

being shocked and laughing with the others. It was only later, when she had spread the blanket out on the sand and lay back, closing her eyes, that the pain of having missed it all began to melt away. She soon fell asleep.

When she woke up a tall muscular boy was standing at the foot of the blanket with another boy, shorter, slight of build, and he, the bigger boy, was saying, "Do you want to play volley ball?"

She sat up and looked about. Her girl friends were at the barbecue pit under the eucalyptus trees about a hundred yards away, getting the lunch ready. Nearby was the volley ball court. There were boys and girls on each side of the net, waiting to play. She rubbed the sleep from her eyes and said, "Yes. I . . . I guess I'd like to play."

When they were crossing the sand to the net, the boy who had asked her to play said his name was Joe and the name of his friend, trailing behind them, was Dennis.

In the living room the whiskey was taking charge. She knew that from the laughing and the silly things they were talking about.

"So tell me again what the conductor said when we got on, Clarence."

"He said, 'You fellas look like you been drinking. We don't allow drunks on the streetcar, you know.'"

"And what'd you say?"

"I said, 'Well, point us to one they do allow 'em on.'"

"God damn!" Joe's laughter shook the house.

With a choked little squeal the little man said, "How about that conductor, Joe?"

Joe laughed again.

"How about that conductor, Joe?"

Joe laughed again.

"Life's a ball, huh, Joe?"

Joe laughed again. "Give me that bottle."

"Funny conductor, eh, Joe?"

Joe only chuckled. Then he said, "I'll kill that kid!"

"Never mind the kid, Joe."

"Don't tell me, 'Never mind.' It's my kid. No good bastard!"

"This Malone's, Joe."

"Nice bar. Like I told you."

"Sure, Joe?"

"Course I'm sure."

"I don't like strange places much."

"Nice. Nice."

She thought of slipping down the stairs by the kitchen and going out through the garage to warn Francis. She would meet him when he pulled up in front of the house. But, no, he knew it was Friday. He was smart. When he caught sight of his angry father, he would toss the keys at him and flee. He would stay gone until his father left for Malone's. Like Sheila Francis didn't fight Joe. His responses were instinctive: mostly he ran.

She took a pan of vegetables from the refrigerator—already cooked, needing only to be heated—and put them on the burner behind the fish. Joe, if he stayed to eat, would complain about the supper, as he did nearly every night. She'd listen to him silently, putting up with it. Sometimes she spoke back to him, saying things so old, so empty—"Get your own meals then." "I'll not cook for you anymore." "How can you enjoy food with so much whiskey in your stomach?"—that she'd later shake her head in wonder that she hadn't thought of something better, more biting, to say. Now she went to the kitchen doorway and asked, "Does ·your friend want supper?"

"What do you think?"

"Please tell me."

"You think I'd ask him out here and not have him eat?"

Clarence said, "Now, listen, Joe, I'm not that hungry."

"You're eating." Then, louder, directed toward the kitchen. "Hear?"

So she'd put out an extra plate. The food was meant

to be eaten. There was plenty for all of them. Maybe Joe
didn't know it but she wanted his friend to stay. This
Clarence was polite, at least polite. She could do with
more of that around here.

"Hey. Your glass is still full. What you quittin' for?"

"Not quitting, Joe. Just taking a little breather."

Gurgle gurgle gurgle. "Here. Put some more in your
glass."

"Got any milk, Joe?"

"Milk?"

"I got to have a glass of milk, Joe."

"In the kitchen."

"Be right back."

"Milk? For Christ sake!"

The little man ran across the kitchen sideways, smiling
and bowing. "Sorry," he said. "I've got to have some
milk. Is it . . . okay?"

She nodded and started to move to the refrigerator.

He put up his hand like a traffic cop and went to the
refrigerator himself. Keeping his eyes on her most of the
time, he opened the door, removed a carton of milk, got
a clean glass at the side of the sink, and filled it. He took
a few swallows, stopped, bowed to her, gestured with the
glass and said, "Nice wife."

She smiled.

He finished the milk and returned to the living room.
Sheila heard him say, "Nice wife you got there, Joe."

"What did you want the milk for?"

"Ulcers, Joe. Bad."

"What about the beer?"

"Been working in breweries all my life. Used to it."

"Yeah?"

"That's right, Joe."

"That god damn kid!"

Once before he had brought home a friend. He and the
friend had gone to Malone's. Early the next morning,
when he had returned alone from the tavern, he had

awakened her and charged her with treating his friend like an unwelcome bum. Then he had gotten into bed and made love to her.

Sheila appreciated Clarence's repeated compliment. Now she called up to Joe: "Maybe your friend wants some cheese and crackers."

"Have some cheese and crackers," Joe said. "Fix your stomach up for some more drinking before we eat."

Clarence came back from the living room, stopped in the doorway, bowed and said, "Just a couple, if you don't mind."

"Won't take a minute."

He stepped into the kitchen.

She opened the cupboard above the stove and removed the crackers, then went to the refrigerator for the cheese. Impulsively she wanted to take him by the hand and lead him to one of the chairs. She wanted to take the cheese and crackers and put them in his mouth. She wanted to hold his hand while he ate. She felt giddy, as though she too were a little drunk. She did not take Clarence's hand, but she enjoyed imagining herself doing it.

"May I help?"

"No," she said.

Watching her he seemed to relax a little. "I don't have a wife," he said. It was like a boy saying he didn't have a bicycle when all the other kids on the block had bicycles.

"I'm sorry."

"Oh well."

She took her time with the snack. "Are you new in the city?"

"Oh, yes." He put his glass down next to the bread box and crossed his arms. "From *Mil*waukee," he said, as though there were many other -waukees. "I was fired from my last job for drinking."

Her heart flip-flopped. From the first she had worried that Joe would be fired for drinking. She was sure he

105

would have a hard time getting another job when that
happened. What else could he work at?

"It wasn't a very nice place. They didn't consider I did
my job." As she spread the cheese on the crackers, he
explained the kind of work he did.

All she got out of it was that he stood somewhere and
counted something. It was as much as she'd ever learned
about Joe's duties. She knew only that he sat somewhere
and stirred something. She didn't care much what kind
of work Clarence did, but she did care very much about
talking to him. She knew it was a kind of rebellion
against Joe, her taking the time and attention of his
friend, but she would risk it. "Have another cracker."

"Thank you." He tilted his head to one side and
smiled. "I like you."

She felt a warm tingle. Softly, almost shyly, she said,
"I like you too. It's almost like I know you."

"I never came here before."

"I know that. It's something else." She thought of
trying to explain. She couldn't. She herself wasn't sure
what she meant.

"What the hell's goin' on in there?"

Neither Sheila nor Clarence responded. She handed
him another cracker.

"You don't drink?" Clarence said.

"No." She hoped Clarence sensed from her reply just
how much of Joe's life was closed to her. She hoped he
sympathized.

"It's better you don't drink," he said. He backed toward the hall. "I'd better go up there. Your husband was
nice enough to ask me out." He turned and started for
the living room.

She was angry that Joe had taken him from her. She
had never felt that way about Joe's other friends. She
could have talked to Clarence for a long time, or listened
to him.

She walked to the window. The fog was moving

swiftly into the stairwell. She watched it splash against the window, insisting on its presence. She pictured it swirling over the rest of the block, wrapping itself around the other houses, turning them all—the houses, the back yards, the streets—to its own dull shades. Looking out at it she was sure it would darken the neighborhood all weekend. She closed her eyes.

On the way to movies or basketball games Joe talked about that day at the beach. It was great, he said, the way she'd set up shots for him: time and again topping the ball up so that he, flying forward, leaping, was able to slam it down on the other side of the net for a score. Dennis was usually with them, in the back seat of Joe's old *Plymouth* coupe, without a date of his own, listening. His shyness had been apparent from the first. At the beach that day Sheila had offered to ask one of their friends to drive back to the city with them, but he, standing a few feet behind Joe, had said no, please don't bother. Sheila somehow understood his tagging along with her and Joe. Sometimes, in the car, Joe would kid him about his shyness:

"The kind of girl you want, Den, doesn't even exist." He turned to Sheila, saying, "He wants someone to call him and pick him up and do all the deciding for him and even take care of the expenses."

"That's not true, Joe," Dennis said from the back seat.

"Then why don't you ask one of Sheila's friends to go out?"

"I don't want a date just to be taking someone out."

"You don't know what you want, Den."

At times Sheila wanted to tell Joe to stop picking on him, but she supposed that if the kidding really bothered Dennis he would say something himself, or just give up and not go along with them. After movies or games Joe would drive down to Daly City or some town on the peninsula where they'd have hamburgers and shakes. He did most of the talking. He told Sheila that one of the coaches at Sacred Heart High had come to him and asked him to try out for tackle on the football team. He had said no. He preferred other things. He liked to work on the car and was proud of the way he'd fixed it up. He didn't have time for football or any other sport. When he graduated he was going to work at the brewery for $1.98 an hour which was more than Dennis or a lot of the other guys who planned to go to college would be making even after they got their degrees. Dennis would argue with him about his plans sometimes, talking about the way college prepared you for a variety of jobs: at least if you didn't like the first one, you had enough education to change to another.

"Look," Joe said, "books teach you what other people know. College gets you ready for what *they* want you to do. I want to do it my own way, learn what I need to learn and work where I'm happy. It's *that* simple."

Dennis rarely agreed but often he'd stop arguing, as if certain that he wouldn't change Joe's mind. Joe admitted once that if he were as smart as Dennis in math or science, liked them as much as Dennis, he might have reason to go to college. The same if he liked football enough to play and try for a college athletic scholarship. But his interests were elsewhere. He talked again about the car. He had rebuilt it from a piece of junk so that now he could (and did) hit eighty on the freeway without a tremble. From good paying part-time jobs he had saved several hundred dollars. He'd go on the night shift at the brewery at first so he could work days for extra money. He knew what he wanted. To Sheila that was the most appealing thing about him. He assaulted obstacles the way he had come down on that volley ball at McNear's Beach. Usually, before they reached the city limits on the way back from the hamburgers and shakes, Dennis was asleep in back and she was curled up beside Joe, listening.

One night they were in a crowded movie house and the previews had just come on, Joe said he didn't remember if he'd locked the car. He told Dennis to go and see. Dennis went, and while he was gone someone took his seat at the end of the aisle, next to Joe. "You'd better tell that man the seat is taken," Sheila said, but Joe ignored her, saying Dennis could find a seat in back. Afterwards, before starting down the peninsula, Joe drove Dennis home, letting him believe they weren't going anywhere that night. After he'd let Dennis off in front of his house, Joe started complaining. "I'm getting tired of him coming with us," he said. "He's getting on my nerves." And, finally, "I'm not going to take him with us anymore." Sheila protested but Joe wouldn't listen. He said he'd made up his mind.

Sheila missed Dennis. Joe was moody and often had gone for long periods without talking, sitting low in the driver's seat at a root beer stand, or, if they were at a beach, wandering off alone, maybe finding some friends from the high school, stopping and chatting with them for a while, finally coming back, revived. Alone with her, Dennis had talked about things he didn't bring up when the three were together. Once he explained an algebra equation it had taken him a week to solve; Sheila, thinking the subject odd, had nevertheless listened and then was fascinated; she had never known anyone to get so excited about algebra or any other school subject. He had spoken about the sudden death of his father a few years earlier and about his mother, who had been ill but who now worked full time to see him through high school and to put money aside for when he went to college. He had also talked about the kind of job, electronics engineer, he wanted to get after graduating from college. She, in turn, had spoken to him about things that only bored Joe: the frivolous girls in her class, how she liked parties but always got nervous before they started, and a lot of other things she didn't talk about even to friends like Ellen. Sheila had tried at different times to fix Dennis up with her classmates, but in senior year most of them were going steady. Besides, Dennis had never seemed to want a date.

Now and then, after Joe had ruled Dennis out of the dates, Sheila would ask about him, but Joe would say something like, "He's busy writing letters to the colleges," giving her the impression that he had plenty of things to keep him occupied. No matter. His absence seemed to change the nature of the dates. More and more Joe and Sheila avoided the games and parties and stayed to themselves.

Sometimes they'd start for a movie but never get there, Joe pulling the *Plymouth* up near the polo field in Golden Gate Park where they'd talk for a while and eventually start kissing. Sometimes Sheila backed off, when he got too passionate, too close; but she did so more out of fear of herself than of Joe or of the dangers, physical and spiritual, the nuns time and again warned her and her classmates about. Joe was strong and his movements against her softened her into a desire to experience more. Often, even when she wasn't with him, she wanted to give herself to him, increasingly sensing that in the surrender would be change, the fulfillment she worried so much would never be hers. It was as if in letting him love her she would be able to eradicate all those things about her that had prevented other boys from desiring her. She worried about the conviction, suspecting it was fanciful, but it remained.

One night, when her parents had gone to a dance sponsored by the Longshoreman's Union, of which her father was a member, and she was home taking care of Frankie, someone knocked on the front door. It was a little after eleven. She had been in the living room, cramming for a Latin exam, and she hesitated before going to the door. Thinking it might be Joe, she peeked through the curtain in the bedroom window next to the door. She was surprised to see Dennis, in suntans, an old *Pendleton* shirt and moccasin slippers, looking as if he lived next door, instead of five miles across town, as if he was just stopping to borrow a pencil. She opened the door. He asked if it was all right if he talked to her for a while. Sure, she said, she had to stay awake anyway until her parents got home. He crossed the living room and sat down in her father's overstuffed chair folding his hands over his stomach, gazing up at the mirror over the mantelpiece across the room, but saying nothing. The silence puzzled her. Finally she said, "Do you want me to get you coffee or something?" He shook his head, stirred a bit, then lowered his eyes to her and said, "I don't like not seeing you, Sheila." The statement was so blunt, the sentiment so undisguised, that Sheila was caught off guard and could only think of inane replies— *That's nice. I appreciate it, Dennis. I miss you too.* Joe had never spoken as directly about his feelings toward her, preferring to beat around, kid her, at times harshly, about why he liked to be with her: "You're a stacked broad, Sheila. Otherwise I'd have nothing to do with you." Then he'd slash the air with laughter. Dennis's remark, tone as much as statement, spoke a need that she now knew had been there all along, buried under something else, his friendship for Joe, a learned politeness, something. But here it was in the open. And she didn't know what to do with it. He got up and began to pace about. "I could have called you on the phone," he said, "but I also wanted to see you." Again he stopped, as if everything he said took enormous preparation, was rendered out of pain and had to end quickly: "That's all." He looked at her, as if for help. Finally she said, "I always ask Joe about you. And I, I . . . ." But she couldn't get it out. The difference between him and Joe maybe—Joe said what he wanted which helped her say what she wanted; Dennis waited, unable to say what would have to be said if her feelings were to find words.

111

Only later did she know what she would have said had he, through eyes or gestures, given her some added little encouragement: "There have been times, there are times, when I'd rather be with you than him." He was on his way before she had a chance to begin, apologizing at the door, saying he shouldn't have come, it was really stupid, not fair to Joe, she meanwhile shaking her head—*Don't say that! You've got it backwards! You should have let me know sooner!*—but he was getting none of the message which she couldn't, just couldn't, put into words.

"God damn it, Sheila! Answer me!"

Her eyes snapped toward the living room.

"What time is it!"

She turned instinctively to the clock above the stove. "Five . . . five-fifty," she said softly.

"Speak up!"

She said it loudly.

"Jesus! They don't listen," she heard him say to Clarence. "They never listen. You're lucky you live alone. You don't know how lucky. What good are they, huh? What good?"

Clarence wasn't biting. "I live alone, Joe, and I've got nothing for it. All I do is buy books and radios. It's no better."

"Radios?"

"Twelve, Joe. Only three or four of 'em work. I get mad 'cause it costs so much to fix them so I buy another. That's what I do every time. It's no good, Joe. What good are twelve radios?"

"Better than what I've got. Like the kid. He's got that car packed with punks right now and is gunning it around every neighborhood in this city. I know it. So what do I do when it stops running? Oh, yeah, I can keep it running but the parts cost money too, besides which . . . ."

There was a pantry at the back of the kitchen. It had

a door. She rushed into the pantry and closed the door. She sat down on the backless stool she used to reach for things on the top shelf. With the door closed she could hear only the drone, not the words. She pressed the heels of her hands into the pits of her ears and closed her eyes tightly. Even the drone went away. The memory played tricks. She leaned back against the cupboard door, the base of her skull touching the edge of a protruding shelf. "God," she whispered. It was just a word spoken, once repeated: "God."

Joe's great aunt died, leaving his father a cottage on a hill in the Portrero District, about seven blocks from the Rainier brewery where Joe planned to work. Sheila and Joe had talked about getting married, but always at some distant time, after both graduated from high school and were working, when they had a chance to add to Joe's saved money. Now his father was willing to sell the house to Joe, low down payment, a loan between father and son spread over a long period with low interest. But he'd have to move quickly because the father couldn't afford to keep paying taxes indefinitely. He might sell it to someone else. Joe again began talking to Sheila about getting married. Earlier they had agreed to wait for a year or so, to make sure. Even a year had seemed soon to Sheila. Several times she had tried to talk Joe into trying to complete some courses at City College. Everyone was talking about the importance of college. Even if he ended up at the brewery some extra education might be needed someday. He had no use for college, he reminded her.

At times, instead of going to a movie, they'd drive to the cottage and look it over. There was a driveway but no garage, only a shed on the little yard in back; he'd extend the driveway all the way back so he could put his car next to the shed where he could work on it. There'd still be a lot of room for a garden for her (which he assumed incorrectly she wanted). If they had a child he'd build a sandbox and play area for the sandbox on the other side of the shed.

"Couldn't you rent the house to someone else until we have enough money saved for furniture and other things?"

"You sound like my mother," he said, "afraid to take chances."

"A house isn't everything," she told him, zeroing in on what really troubled her.

"I'm not doing all this for myself," he said angrily.

She doubted him but had reason to deny her doubts. She was afraid, afraid that if she fought him—couldn't he buy the house and rent it to someone else until they were married?—he would leave her, maybe find another. She had come to think of their lives as one. She did not fight him.

One night, late, after he had measured off the little living room for a carpet he was to pick up wholesale at a store that was going out of business, they sat down on the day bed the aunt had left in the room that served as both dining room and living room. He sent his hand up under her sweater and began to massage her bare back with unaccustomed gentleness. She moved warmly toward him. He surrounded her, kissing her, and soon was trying to remove her sweater. She tried to pull away. Don't be afraid, he told her. But she was. She had said she was sure that once they started making love, completely, it wouldn't stop. She said it again:

"We'd better wait."

"I'm married to you now," he said, "except for the piece of paper."

"I feel the same . . . but I just don't want to do anything now." How could she explain, about the house, about what that had done to him, how that frightened her? "Let's go down to the furniture store. It's open late. At least you can look at what they've got, the carpets."

But he ignored her, shouldering her down, sending his hand between her legs, kissing her mouth wetly.

Lying there, eyes fixed on the naked light bulb that shone from the kitchen, she felt him grow hard against her leg, felt the muscles of his arms tightening around her torso. She flinched at the touch of his fingers, pressing sharply into her breasts. Soon she was aware only of his desire. It didn't seem right. She struggled to sit up, couldn't.

"Don't," she said once, but she knew he would, knew there was now no choice. She lay back limply, expecting soon to feel the sweet sinking sensation that she had felt so often in the car, where she had let him work with hands and mouth, taking all but the last.

He moved swiftly, roughly pulling her clothes off, grunting now and then, until finally she lay beneath him naked.

She was watching him, that wild black hair of his illuminated against the kitchen light, expecting him to remove his own clothes.

But he didn't. He opened his pants, lowered her hand and began to rub it over him, telling her to squeeze, hard, and she did, harder than she would have imagined he could bear. In moments he was forcing himself in, chafing the dry lips, punching down, down, until, at the moment of invasion, he spilled hotly into her. She waited. The sweetness would soon envelop her.

The relentless eye shone at her from the kitchen.

He groaned once, then twisted out, pulling himself up. He sat over her, his shoulders rising and falling as he breathed.

She waited. There would be something more.

He got up, went to the kitchen, where he had some days earlier put a pack of beer in the small refrigerator. She heard the refrigerator door open. She heard the cap snap off the bottle. She heard him swallowing. She took her clothes and hurried to the bathroom.

"Sheila!"

She didn't answer.

"Hey!" He was up, thumping through the hall.

She opened the pantry door.

He burst into the kitchen, stopping a foot or so from her. "Where is he? I want an answer!"

"He's not late."

He stepped forward, bumping against her. "I said five-thirty. I said be here at five-thirty."

"You said six." She was looking at the window.

"No, god damn it! Five-thirty!"

"Six."

He slapped her, a loud stinging slap.

She held her cheek but said nothing.

"Bitch!"

Clarence was in the doorway. "What's the matter?"

"Never mind," Joe said, inhaling deeply. His face was an angry crimson. He turned to Sheila and glared at her for a moment. Then he left the kitchen.

Clarence remained. "What's the matter?" he said to Sheila.

"Get out of here," she whispered.

Clarence did not budge. Now he was frowning. "I heard a slap. Joe hit you, didn't he?"

She shook her head.

Joe had come back. He was standing behind Clarence. "What are you doing?"

Clarence turned. "I don't like that, Joe."

"Don't like what?"

"Nobody should hit a wife."

"Please," Sheila said to Clarence, but it was too late.

Joe slapped his open hands against the front of the little man's shirt, squeezed, then raised Clarence off the floor. He pulled him close, so that his face nearly touched Clarence's. He laughed into Clarence's face.

Clarence was suspended in air. His head was half buried in his khaki work shirt. His feet dangled a few inches above the floor. Still he spoke calmly: "I know what it means."

"Know what what means?"

"Hitting a woman. You're a coward. Put me down."

"You're crazy." Joe laughed again.

"Put him down," Sheila said, surprising herself.

Joe turned, astonished. He dropped Clarence and started toward her, raising his thick arm.

Clarence stumbled, caught his balance, came up behind Joe, and, with a movement of hand so fast that Sheila could barely see it, clipped Joe between the shoulder blades.

"Gaagh!" Joe's arms went out. Simultaneously his shirt front, barely tucked in beneath his big belly, popped out. "What the hell?" It was surprise, not anger.

The little man looked at Joe's back. "It's not right."

Joe turned on him.

"Leave him alone," Sheila said.

Joe looked from one to the other.

Neither of them moved.

He spun toward Sheila.

Quickly Clarence stepped around him and put himself in front of her.

Joe caught him in the face with the back of his hand, and Clarence went to the floor. He swung around, arms out, and thrust Sheila against the table.

She pushed herself away and stood defiantly before him. "You've done enough," she said. "You've done enough."

Clarence had pulled himself off the floor. His nose was bleeding. He took a dirty handkerchief from his pocket and held it to his nose.

Joe, confused, turned from him to Sheila, then back.

"A man shouldn't hit his wife," Clarence said. He didn't seem to be speaking to anyone in particular. "No, sir." He staggered out of the kitchen and into the hall.

"Hey, mouse, come back here."

117

He kept going.

Joe went after him. "Come here, you funny little bastard. Just some family fun. It's over now. Have a drink."

The front door opened. "Maybe I shouldn't interfere in people's families," Clarence said. "But you shouldn't hit your wife, Joe."

"I quit hitting her. C'mon, let's forget it."

"I can't drink with you anymore, Joe."

"Wait!"

The front door closed.

Joe rumbled toward it, got there, opened it. "Hey! Hey!" His voice echoed through the enclosed stairway, but no one replied. "Little bastard!" he shouted, then slammed the door.

Sheila braced herself for the worst. He would come flying into the kitchen, blaming her for driving off his new friend. He might strike her again.

But he did not fly into the kitchen; he came slowly. She looked up to see his hulking body in the doorway. He was wheezing. His tobacco-stained teeth showed. His dark eyes were fixed on her. He said nothing. He did not even advance toward her.

The *Pontiac* rattled to a stop in front of the house.

Like a great sleeping beast alerted by the sound of a small animal in a nearby thicket, Joe raised his head and listened. Fire rose up in his eyes. He made a little growling sound and turned anxiously toward the front of the house. In a moment he was racing through the hall, shouting, "I'll kill him!"

There was a party. Dennis was there. Dennis had a girl friend. No, but was with a girl. Someone had moved the dining room furniture and they were dancing in the dining room. Ellen's house, or was it Sheila's cousin's house? Dennis asked her to dance. He spoke easily this time. They were all drinking, a lot of beer, but the boys

mainly, and there was punch, spiked punch. Everyone
was drinking. The party was for her and Joe, and Dennis
had come to her and when they were dancing . . . Joe
was shouting at him. Joe was shouting and then Dennis
and Joe were arguing but the rest . . . . Two boys helped
Dennis. On the floor? Yes. Joe was pulling her away
from him and then the two boys were picking him up.
   "I don't want to go!"
   "We're going!"
   "What did you do to him? What did you do?"
   "Get your coat!"
   "Answer me, Joe! Answer me!"
   "Get your coat, I said!"

She moved dizzily to the stove. She reached uncer-
tainly for the chair, got it, pulled it under her, went
slowly down. She reached out and turned on one of the
knobs on the stove. With a staccato pop several little
fingers of bluish-orange flame rose up from the first
burner, surrounding the bottom of the frying pan. She
turned back the knob. The flames flattened. She turned
the knob forward a bit. The flames reached sporadically
up, then receded into a quivering bluish glow. She did
the same with the second burner, until she had it right.
She pushed her chair back and looked at the flames,
flickering at first but then holding, steady, blue.

Dennis came to the cottage. It must have been a
couple of months later. It was brave of him. Joe was
at work but the man across the street, a friend of his
father, others, might tell Joe. There were marks over his
right eye from the stitches. She made him coffee and
heated the packaged pastries she'd gotten at the grocery
store that morning. She sat with him on the porch, a tiny
porch in front. She shouldn't have let Joe do it, he said.
She should have waited. Now how could she know, about
Joe, herself? Time would tell, she said. Time? Yes. He

nodded to that. He hoped it was true, he said. He spoke so calmly. He asked her if it would hurt her stomach to take a walk to the little playground at the top of the hill. She laughed. It reminded her of the way he'd reach past her to get the door of the coupe open for her when the three of them had gone places together, as if she had no strength at all. No, she told him, she could walk all the way downtown and it wouldn't hurt her. So they walked up and stood by the fence, looking out through the haze toward the factories in South City, seeing the tips of the towers of the Bay Bridge, watching the cars racing each other down a nearby freeway. They didn't speak on the way up. They stopped at the swings on the way back and she got on and he pushed her. "Higher," she said. He made her sail up so far she felt as if she might cata-pult out over the houses and go sailing across the sky. She cried out once, when the swing went so high the chain snapped and she nearly fell. He didn't push as hard then. Finally she got off and they walked down the hill. There was a small red convertible parked in front of the cottage, in it a tanned blonde girl she'd never seen be-fore. Earlier he'd said, "Someone is going to pick me up." Now he introduced them. The girl was maddeningly pretty. Sheila expected to feel a flash of resentment, the kind she so often felt just looking at a face like that, but it didn't come. She kept smiling at the girl, wanting to say something pleasant to her, as if to make up for the cuts she had given to others like her. But she could think of nothing. She waved at them as they pulled away and was happy, inexplicably happy for Dennis.

"I'm going, Sheila!" He was back in the house. "Do you hear? I don't want supper. You tell him I'll kill him! Hear! Tell him he was late!" Banging through one of the rooms. "He was, you bitch!" Down the hall then, toward the front door. "Was!"

The fire was her fault. She had started stew meat simmering in a pan and left the dish towel on the stove. She wanted to measure off the little square where the sandbox was to be put. She had told Joe it could wait; the baby wouldn't be able to use it for months after it was born; but he insisted. She found a yardstick in the shed and came out, kneeling with difficulty because her stomach was so large, to begin the measurements. She heard the noise. She looked over to see the glass in one of the panes in the kitchen window begin to crack, looking as though an invisible hand were scribbling on it with tremendous speed, cracking in a thousand places it seemed. Before she could rush across the yard the window burst open. Then another went, another, and soon all of them, and the flames poured up into the sky. She rushed to the house next door and called the fire department, but the trucks arrived too late.

Her hair quivered, dark and silver, as she bent down and blew out the flames under the frying pan. She pushed the frying pan aside, leaned forward and blew out the pilot flame, then the flames under the pan with the vegetables. She eased back, gazing at one of the burners. Circles of tiny mouths hissed up at her. She closed her eyes. The hissing faded into the low hollow sound of the wind up from the beach, swirling through the passages of the house, swirling and whistling until at last she had enclosed it and it was still.

Donovan, the Cat Man

A couple of them sitting at the other side of the sun room are laughing at me now. It is nothing new. My silences make them laugh. I am funny to look at and I do not talk. Because I do not talk, my doctor suggested I write. He said write about yourself when you were a little boy. It is hard for me to remember when I was a little boy. That was a long time ago, nearly fifteen years. Sometimes things come back though.

The law student over there is nearly ready to be released. Yesterday he told us at group meeting that his mother came and brought him a pair of shoes. He said he told her to take the shoes away. Some of the patients congratulated him. Afterwards the doctor told the group that Mr. Haas. That is his name. Has progressed very well. I am sure we will all miss him when he leaves he said.

Sometimes Mr. Haas speaks to me. Sometimes I want to speak to him. He and his friend have been laughing at me. I think he is going to speak to me pretty soon.

I am at the ping pong table. There are windows all around the room but the ones near the ping pong table have the best view. I just looked out at the city. All those brightly painted wooden Victorian mansions around the hospital. Green park with children. Beyond them the low even white rows of attached stucco houses sloping toward the beach. Clear sky and the ocean all white-capped.

Mr. Haas came over. He said, "What are you doing Mr. Donovan?"

I did not turn from the window. I did not know what to say. I did not know what to tell him. I am writing. He could see that.

He spoke to his friend. "Mr. Donovan doesn't speak to anyone," he said. "Except his psychiatrist. Isn't that right Mr. Donovan?"

I nodded.

"When I first came here you frightened me. You know that?"

I remembered the night. His mother brought him. He was drunk and smoking a cigar. He kept pointing at my head and saying that's so big I think I'm in hell. When his mother left he tried to climb into a black circle in one of the squares of linoleum. He kept calling it mother. That was a few months ago. Now he is well.

"Don't you care about anything?" he said. "Don't you want to get well?"

I nodded.

"No you don't. Otherwise you would speak to people. You just sit by yourself all the time."

I do not want to sit by myself. I want to speak. I want to get well.

"You make everyone uncomfortable. Why can't you try to be friendly?"

I saw a child lying on the grassy slope of the park across from the hospital. His head was turned sideways with his cheek against the grass. Above him other children were playing in a sandbox. Beyond the sandbox was a bench where several mothers sat chatting. No one seemed to notice the child alone.

"You think it was easy for me to come through a breakdown and get myself oriented again? It wasn't, you know. I had to work at it."

The child lay very still. I wondered what he was watching. Maybe a ladybug. Once I found a ladybug with a lavender back instead of an orange one. I put it in my pocket and took it home to my mother. It was dead.

"I just told the new patient Mr. Brook that he would have to work hard to get well. Then I looked at you. You are ridiculous. You don't even try. You just sit around with your funny head looking ridiculous."

My mother said throw that thing out. What do you put dead bugs in your pocket for? What else have you got in there? She found a peanut in a shell that had been through the wash. And a pocket watch I had found in my father's bureau drawer after he was dead. She put it in the cupboard. I cried. Having the watch with me was like having my father. My father had died on his way home from work or something. The watch did not work but it reminded me of him. I must have had a tantrum. My mother locked me in my room until supper.

"I would like to introduce you to Mr. Brook. But what would that do but depress him. You have been here months and have not improved at all. What is he to think about the hospital?"

I think I tried to kill another boy on our block about then. He said I had never had a father. Big head bastard is what he called me. He and his friends. They threw rocks at me. I hid in the back yard. Sometimes I hid in the apple tree. One day he and his friends came down the driveway looking for me. They could not find me and were leaving when one of them looked up in the tree and saw me. They all started to throw rocks. One hit me above the eye. They were below me now. I dropped down on the leader. He fell to the ground. I saw a stone. Bigger than the ones they were throwing. I picked it up and began beating him on the head. His arms started wiggling. The other boys pulled me off.

"The two of us have been sitting over there making fun of you. What do you think of that?"

The leader was hurt. He was taken to the hospital with a brain concussion. His mother came to our house and told my mother she was going to have the other mothers sign a petition that I be kept locked up. You hear that my mother said. When the lady left she beat me and called her cousin who was a priest. He came and talked to me about an orphan school for boys. He said if I did anything else like that he would see that I was sent there. And I would not see my mother again. I hid in the basement. I could hear them talking. Him and my mother. In the kitchen. I could not tell what they were saying.

"If you want to know what I think, I think you shouldn't be here. They should isolate you at the state hospital so you wouldn't be a bad influence on other patients." Now he turned to Mr. Brook. "See," he said, "he's harmless. Come on over." Mr. Brook came over and stood beside the ping pong table.

I stayed away from the children on the block after that. When I was in school I made friends. I played one o'cat and pinky in the school yard at recess and lunchtime. The other boys let me catch. Often the bell rang before I got my ups. Later when I stayed after school I got my ups after everyone else. The boy who ran the games told sister I was a good catcher.

"That head is liable to scare you at first. But after you get used to it you don't mind so much," Mr. Haas said to Mr. Brook. "Bawhh!" Mr. Haas opened his hands and pushed them toward me.

I flinched.

"See. Nothing to be afraid of. All this silence of his is just bluff. Nothing to be afraid of."

"Stop," I said.

"So now you want to talk."

I turned away.

"Tell us what you are writing then."

I put my hand over my notebook.

"Let's see." He tried to pull it away.

I held it tight. I drew back my other hand and made a fist.

Mr. Brook ran out of the room.

"Come back," said Mr. Haas. "He won't do anything."

But Mr. Brook was gone.

He glared at me. "See that? You make everyone uncomfortable." He yanked the notebook from me and threw it on the floor. "What does it matter what you're writing?"

We played another school in softball. The boys on the other team laughed at me. Father McCarthy who drove us in his station wagon put his arm around me and said don't pay any attention to them. Some batters kicked dirt in my face when Father McCarthy the umpire wasn't looking. Let's fight them the captain of our team said. No said Father McCarthy. Don't pay attention. We won the game. I did not go to the games with other schools after that.

"A book I suppose. A creature like you could write a book."

I read after that. I don't remember what except that they were stories. Animal stories at first. Then sports stories. Then war stories. But I did not do well in high school. My mother moved to San Francisco and sent me to a Jesuit school. I barely got by. That's what she always told people. He barely gets by. I don't know what's to become of him. One day I was reading a war story in history class when the prefect of discipline came in to announce that it was time for weekly confessions. He saw me reading. He shouted you pig you swine you bore you slob stand up. The other boys laughed. He kept calling me names. The boys laughed every time he spoke. He called more names. I thought he would expel me from school. But when I went to his office that afternoon all he made me do was make me write a thousand word composition on why there is fuzz on a tennis ball. I enjoyed writing it. After that the other boys called me Pighead. I do not have a face like a pig but my head is as big as a pig's.

"Is that what it is? A book?"

I nodded.

He picked up the notebook.

I tried to take it from him.

He pulled away.

When I was in my third year of high school I wrote a story about a lavender ladybug. It won first prize in the school magazine contest. I forget what the story was about but I remember it had something to do with the ladybug I found when I was little.

"Let me read it," he said.

I grabbed the notebook from him.

"God damn you. That's why you'll never get well."

I hit him.

His nose was bleeding when he left the room.

"I'm sorry," I said.

The boys in the sand pile stood and began calling. The boy on the slope remained still. The boys in the sand pile began looking around the park. Finally they found him. They rushed down the hill and stood over him. He did not move. They kept looking. I don't know if he got up at all. A social worker came and took me out of the sun room before I could see.

My doctor said what did you hit him for. I think he asks me questions because one time he hopes to catch me by surprise and I will answer. I want to answer sometimes. I even know what I want to say. But I can't find the words. Not even the word to start with. I think of yes. It turns into and. Then into something else. Then into something that is not even a word. Like nyend. I know I will be foolish if I speak. I also know he won't laugh. But it won't make any difference. If I know.

He said, "Does it trouble you that Mr. Haas will be leaving soon?"

I shook my head.

"What caused you to hit him?"

My mother said you may as well go to college. You can't do anything else, not even go in the Army. I don't want you sitting around the house forever. I wish you had an interest. You just mope around. Nothing is solved unless you get interested. Why don't you take up a hobby or something.

"He was only trying to get you to speak, was he not?"

A cat came in our house. My mother was still at work and I was cooking supper. I had to open the door because of the smoke. The cat came in. With a lot of colors, brown and gray but mainly white. He walked up to my leg and rubbed himself against my leg. I gave him some hamburger. He finished it. Then he climbed up next to the bread box and lay down and looked at me.

"What are you writing?"

I went on a streetcar to take a class at the university at night. They have classes at night for people who work. I took composition. You were supposed to take that first. I wanted to write something again. I knew I could write a lot taking that. On the way home I thought I would write about the cat. He was still staying with us. Sometimes he sounded like he was talking.

"Francis?"

I said go put your head down and he did. Right where he was standing when I said it. At night he came to my bed. I could hear him calling when I woke up. It sounded like out. But it sounded different at other times. Sometimes like milk. When he wanted to have something to drink. I listened all the time. He was saying things. No. I thought he was though. I said things back. Sometimes I said what, to see if he'd say what he had just said all over again. Sometimes he did. Sometimes I said do you want to go out and he said nyp. Like he was saying nope. That was when he didn't want to go out. Sometimes he said mmnnyaa. Like yeah. Then I opened the door and he went out.

"What would you prefer to do? Show me what you are writing or speak to me?"

He has to play tricks. That shows what he thinks of me. Once he was outside this room talking to the head nurse. I walked by. I walk funny. I do that because of my head. I pull it way back so it seems smaller. Also I take short steps so it doesn't bounce. People don't laugh as much when I walk that way. I went into the TV room and looked back. Sneaking my eyes back. He was lifting his feet in tiny steps. Imitating me. The nurse was smiling. Then she put her hand on her mouth. I could see her eyes. Still smiling. That was a time I almost talked. Said to the doctor why are you doing that. But I didn't.

The cat followed me. He always followed me. When I went to the store to get things for supper. Mac the grocery man said is that your cat out there by the vegetables. I looked out the window. He was sitting under a box. Playing with a tassle of corn hanging down. I said yes. He said keep that god damn cat away from my boxes. I tried to keep him home. But he always jumped out at the front door. Between my legs. I didn't want to lock him in a room. I took him. In Mac's I carried him in my arms.

"You know, there's a chance we can get you a job when you're better. In the afternoons at first. Then all day when you are used to it. Would you like that?"

I worked in an art gallery on Bush Street. Gallatin's. That was after I was at college. No. When I was there. In the days. Then I went to the composition class at night. Two nights a week. That's when something happened. When my cat. No. That was before. Something else.

"Of course, first we'd have to understand, you'd have to understand, why you hit Mr. Haas. We could hardly ask an employer to take you on if you were liable to hit someone."

Today I saw Mr. Haas in the sun room. He smiled at
me. He showed me a model boat he was making. An old
ferry boat like the kind that used to go to Sausalito
before the bridge was built. He said I've been wanting to
show you this. Like nothing happened. I looked at it. I
looked so he wouldn't say you aren't interested in anything. Then his words would peck at me all day. So I
looked at it. He said I am going to buy myself a boat
when I get out of here. I thought he'd make fun of me.
I thought he'd say you can never run a boat. It takes
brains to run a boat. Something. Later I got mad. I got
mad because he wanted to show me something. It was
like he was saying look how easily I show you things.
Why can't you show me what you are writing?

"So why don't we get back to just what angered you?"

I got off the streetcar. They were laughing. I always
get nervous when I hear a lot of people laughing. Especially boys. Listening to their hard voices. It is like they
have discovered they have strong voices all the time and
have to use them. When I was little. When we lived
where we had the apple tree. They used to scream at me.
They laughed when I shouted back. I wanted to run over
and. Then I saw they were looking at something by the
streetcar track. I was across the street looking at them.
Then I looked up the track. And saw. A cat. Its head was
cut off. The part with no head was on one side of the
track. I ran over. The head on the other. I picked him
up. My cat. They were pointing at me and laughing. I
was crying. Looking at the head in one hand. The body
in the other. The eyes were open. I could see his teeth.
Stop it I shouted. Stop it I shouted. They were still laughing. But they were backing up. That's all I said. Stop it.
Stop it.

"You put that notebook under the mattress of your
bed at night, don't you?"

How does he know that?

"If, instead, you left it on the table beside the bed or,

better, with me, I could read what you have written. Then we could spend our time together more profitably."

Sometimes I feel like he will get up and grab it from me. Then I will hit him. Maybe. The way I hit Mr. Haas.

"It would be much easier, however, if you tried to read me a passage. Or hand it to me now and let me read. Would that be so terrible?"

I won't answer.

"Why?"

The teacher said I would like to have your assignment dittoed. We can discuss it next week. I told him I didn't want him to. He said it is curious. Interesting. He said many papers by freshmen don't exhibit a sense of style. He said yours does. He said there are numerous grammatical errors. We can discuss those too. Everyone was gone. We were in the classroom alone. The lights in the hall were out already. There was just the light in the classroom. I was sitting in a desk in front. He was behind the teacher's desk. I kept saying please don't. That made him want to use it more. I said I don't want anyone else to read it. He said writing is for communication. Why would a person write if he didn't want others to read it. He said suppose Mark Twain threw *Huckleberry Finn* away after he wrote it. He said not every student has the opportunity to have his work used for group discussion. I kept saying no. He said it's late. I don't have time to debate with you about this. He said I'm going to use it. You can take that as an assignment. After that I didn't go back.

My mother said not going. For God sake. You've only started. You have no will power. What have I raised. She kept saying that. What have I raised. I had the job at Gallatin's. She didn't say anything about that. She said it would be different if you'd failed. She sat at the kitchen table. She put her head down. She put her hands on top of her head. She said what have I raised. I remember that. What have I raised?

"Why?"

I got up. I went over. I started hitting his desk with my fist. I hit it again and again. I wanted to hit him. He would make them keep me in my room if I did that. I looked up. He was sitting back in his chair watching me. Not afraid. I hit it and got tired. My notebook was on the floor.

"Are you finished now, Mr. Donovan?"

I think everything he does is a trick. I think it was a trick when he said that. I got down and picked up my notebook. It was like when I picked up my cat. I looked at the doctor. I said, "You killed my cat!"

He said, "What cat?"

I have been in my room since they gave a party for Mr. Haas. My doctor was there. He wouldn't see me in the office anymore. It was because I hit his desk and wouldn't speak. He said he would see me again when I controlled myself. He said then we would try talking about a job again. Maybe.

I was working up front in Gallatin's. A man came in by himself and started talking in front of the painting of a green twig. Mr. Gallatin wasn't there and neither was his niece. I had to stand in front when they weren't there and watch people. I don't remember what the man said. He wasn't talking to me. To himself. I got frightened. When that happens my hands shake. He saw them shaking. He saw me. He stopped talking to himself. He came over and said if I believed they weren't all acting I'd stop that. I said who. He said the doctors. He said I am smarter than they are. He said I know there is something wrong when I tell Eleanor things though she is dead. He said I know something is wrong when people look at me and get alarmed. But I don't believe any of the reasons they give me because I am smarter than them and I know they are acting. He had a thin moustache and was tall and for some reason he looked French to me. Then he walked out. I worried after that. I was afraid when I was alone someone like him would walk in again. If he hadn't walked out I wouldn't have known what to do.

Mr. Haas's girl friend came to the party.

"This is Mr. Donovan," he said.

"Oh?"

"The one I told you about."

She nodded like he didn't have to say more.

I kept looking at her. She had long legs with very dark stockings, almost black. Her brown hair fell down over one eye. She moved her arm gracefully when she shoved the hair back. I could not stop looking at her.

"So," said Mr. Haas.

She was looking at me.

"So." He wanted me to go away.

I did not go away.

Mr. Haas was looking around me for someone else to introduce her to. But I kept looking at her. She looked at me but not like others have done. She was trying to see something in my face. I knew I shouldn't think that. But I did. She was not seeing just my ugliness. I wanted the lights to go out. Then I would reach out and touch her.

On my lunch hour at Gallatin's I went into a department store. A girl was trying on beads. I stood behind and looked at her. She saw me in the little mirror. She smiled at me in the mirror. I smiled back. She held up two strings of beads. Which ones do you like, she said into the mirror. I said the dark ones. She said so do I. She put the others down. She put the dark ones around her neck. She said snap them on for me will you. I went up close to her. She was holding the beads. Waiting for me to take them. I wanted to rub my hand up and down on her soft sweater. I stood there looking at her soft sweater and then her soft hair. She held the beads behind her neck for me to take them. I did. I snapped them on.

I stood close while she looked in the mirror. My head in
the mirror looked like a bear's head. She was so pretty.
These are the ones she said. I thought she would turn
around. But she didn't. Her face moved away and she
walked to the end of the counter to pay the salesgirl. I
stood watching. When she started for the door I said
wait. She turned around:

"What do you want?"

"Can I help you get something else?"

"I'm . . . I'm going home."

"Maybe we can just look at some other things."

I didn't know how to say what I wanted to. I wanted
to go to different departments and pretend I was buying
her things. Coats and dresses. Look at her in them after
she had tried them on. I couldn't think of how to say it
so I just looked at her. She said why are you looking at
me? I didn't answer. She turned to a lady behind a nearby
counter. She said will you please call the floor manager.
I turned around, looking for someone I could pretend I
was with. So I wouldn't seem so strange. There was no
one. I hurried to the escalator. I went up. I found a fat
woman on the next floor, looking at sheets. I stood beside her. She didn't seem to notice me. I stayed close to
her until she went out of the store. I thought someone
would come up and arrest me. No one did.

It looked like she was waiting for me to say something.

After my mother died I stayed alone in the house. I
didn't go out even for food. A neighbor came in one day
because I hadn't been going out. I hadn't shaved or anything and was sitting on the floor. He spoke to me. I
couldn't speak back. I remember him speaking but I
couldn't speak back. I remember I couldn't think of anything to say. I remember I was dizzy. Then I was taken
here.

"Would you like a mint?" She held a green box out.

I put my hand out and she dropped a mint into it.

Mr. Haas was on the other side of the sunroom saying

to Mr. Brook I want you to meet Mavis. That is her name.

She said, "I'll bet I could get you to speak."

I imagined her knowing all the reasons I couldn't speak. I imagined her touching me in an odd way, maybe only on the forehead, and getting rid of my fear of speaking.

"Mavis?"

She didn't look across at Mr. Haas. She said I am speaking to Mr. Donovan. She stopped. She looked at me. I was smiling. She saw. I think she saw I wanted her to stay with me. We both laughed. The doctor came over. He must have met her before. He spoke to her. He didn't look at me. He talked about Mr. Haas. How quickly he had gotten well. The doctor did not speak to me but when he walked away he put his hand lightly on my shoulder. I think he was trying to let me know he was still disciplining me but also liked me. I didn't like him not speaking to me. I would have liked it even if he had spoken angrily. I was glad he went away.

"Is there some place we can sit down? This room is so crowded."

I nodded.

"Take me there."

No one was in the TV room. But if I walked down the hall with her someone would say something. Maybe Mr. Haas would shout at me. That would have made me stop. And run from her. Maybe I would do something stupid. Maybe I would shout back. Or maybe I would hit him again. She held out her hand. I didn't take it. I went out of the sunroom. If she was going with me she would have to follow. I wanted her to come to the TV room but I couldn't walk out with her. She would have to understand. I went out, wanting her to follow. Hoping she would.

Geraldine always wore black dresses. She was Mr. Gallatin's niece. She made diagrams before we got the pictures ready for display. There was a partition between the gallery in front and the work area in back. In back I held up the paintings one by one and she sat at a table opposite. That's where she made diagrams. When she had it the way she wanted we went up front and hung the paintings according to the diagram. Sometimes she was the only one I spoke to all day. I usually didn't speak to customers. When she or Mr. Gallatin were up front I was in back working on mountings or something else. Sometimes Mr. Gallatin didn't come in. My mother said why don't you get a job that pays good money. I knew I should get another job but I liked working with Geraldine. She wasn't as pretty as Mr. Haas's girl friend but she was pretty. I told her what happened to my cat. She said the best things are always lost, Francis. When I was sad about something I thought of what she said.

I heard someone walking down the hall behind me.

Once she was sitting behind the table and I was holding pictures. Her feet got hot so she took off her shoes. She was sitting with her legs crossed holding the diagram. She was moving her leg up and down, up and down. I tried not to look but I kept looking. She walked around in her stockings all that day. Except when a customer came in up in front. Mr. Gallatin wasn't at work that day. She used to talk more when he wasn't there. She talked a lot that day. And she walked around light-footed and cheerful. Pretty soon all I could think about were her legs. Even when I wasn't looking at them. The shape of them and the way they moved. I had said very little. Near the end of the day we were in back working with the last of the paintings. I tried to think of how to say what I was thinking. About her legs. Everything I thought of seemed ridiculous. You have nice legs Geraldine. I can't stop looking at your legs. Everything. But the more I couldn't say something the more I looked at them. Pretty soon I was trembling inside. Finally I burst out and said I want to touch them. She said what. I said your legs. They're so beautiful. I just want to rub my hands on them. She had been holding the diagram up, studying something. She lowered it to her lap. She said would that make you feel good Francis. I nodded. I almost dropped the painting I was holding. She put the diagram on the floor and said come here. I put the painting down. I walked over. She stretched her legs out. Her heels touched the floor. She raised her skirt a little. I stared at her legs. I felt myself going down. I had to hold the side of the chair I was shaking so much. I just looked at her legs. "Well, touch me then." I slid my hand up. Over her knees. Up under her skirt. She wasn't looking. Her head was back. I kept my hand moving up. She opened her legs a little. I felt the rough surface of her stockings. Then I felt where the stockings stopped and her legs were bare. She opened her legs a little more. With my forefinger I touched the soft cloth between her legs. It was burning hot. I could hear her breathing. I rubbed my forefinger up and down over the soft cloth. "Stop now," she said. I didn't want to stop. I put my hand. The palm of my hand. Hard against the depression under the soft cloth. Her legs snapped together. She shoved her chair back. "Stop now!" Her fists were in her dress where I'd been touching. She was looking at me. Her face was red. "You have to stop now!" I felt myself hard. I couldn't stand up. "Francis!" I got up and turned away quickly so she wouldn't see me sticking out. I went back and got the painting. I held it. Kneeling down. Until I wasn't hard anymore. She began to work with the diagram. Once I said her name. It just came out. I wanted to go back and touch her some more. I think she could tell that from the way I said her name. She said we have to work, Francis. And we worked. I didn't touch her after that.

There was no one else in the room. Only the light from the outside shone through the long window over the street. I was sitting in a lounge chair facing the door when she opened it and came in behind me. I could feel her standing behind my chair. Then she walked around and pushed the lounge chair beside me around in front of me. She sat down. Our knees were almost touching. I looked away.

"I teach first graders," she said. "When they start school they are afraid like you. Do you know that?"

I shook my head.

"Vern." That's Mr. Haas. "Told me about you. About how you wouldn't talk. Even to your doctor. I told him I thought I could get you to talk. Do you think I can?"

I didn't like her saying that to Mr. Haas. But I nodded. I was sure she was someone I could talk for. I wanted to talk. I wanted to say how nice she looked to me. I wanted to say. I couldn't say anything. I couldn't even look at her. Her fingers were massaging my hands. I was nodding. I kept nodding. Hoping she knew I wanted her to stay there. Even if I wasn't able to talk. "Why must you be so shy? If you could relax I could help you. It's not difficult if you're not afraid." I reached out. It was so dark. I put my hand on her dress. I could feel her breasts. My hand was in the depression between them. I thought of pulling my hand away but I didn't. It was like the cat. When I touched him between his neck and his back. I heard myself groaning. She put her hand on mine. She was lowering my hand, trying to. I kept it there. She tried hard to push it away. I kept it there. "Mr. Donovan!" The light went on. "What are you doing?" It was Mr. Haas. I pulled my hand away and my chair slid back. "You," he shouted. "You!" He came at me. I was already sliding to the floor. I put my hands up to the sides of my head. I knew he was going to hit me. He kicked me instead. In the chest. On the side of my stomach. Then I forget. I just remember the kicks. "I told you he was hopeless!" He tried to kick my head but my hands were protecting me. My eyes were closed but when he kicked I saw silver bursts of light. I don't know how long he kicked. I remember when he stopped he was breathing heavily over me. I saw their legs in front of me. She said you shouldn't have done that Vern. He helped me up. He put me in the lounge chair. He was holding me in the lounge chair. She was angry at him. She said he didn't hurt me. She said now they won't let you go when you're supposed to go. He was holding me hard against the chair. Yes they will, he said. He looked at me. He said to me you won't tell what I did. I'll say you attacked her. He kept holding me. Looking down. Saying do you hear me. I nodded. As they left he turned off the light. She said he's harmless Vern. You shouldn't have kicked him. I waited awhile. Then I got up and went to my room. My side hurt when I walked.

The door is open. I hear them in the sunroom. Having the party. There is laughter. A lot of laughter. I have curled up very tightly. With my upper legs against my stomach. My side is not as painful this way. I can write this way. They are still laughing.

The Thumping of the Grass

It was a vacant lot, I remember that, and they used to burn it out every summer. My brother and I watched from our bedroom window, afraid to go up by the trucks or the firemen. What keeps coming back has to do with the lot and it comes back in dreams, the ones I remember, the ones I have just before waking, and I am in the lot with a girl only the girl is my brother which in the dream seems natural but not natural now that I say it.

There was a real girl and she lived in a dirty yellow house beyond our back fence and after my brother died I saw her kissing a big boy in the vacant lot and it embarrassed me but I watched. It was like somebody getting beaten the way he came down over her with his heavy arms and brought her hard to the ground and made her whimper.

Her name was Sylvia and one day I rode my bike around the block and saw her sitting on one of the three steps in front of the yellow house's screened-in porch reading comic books and maybe waiting for the big boy and I looked away, afraid my eyes would tell her what I knew about her in the lot but she saw me and said "Come here" and I did.

Her knees were up so high I could see part of her thick white thighs under her skirt and she said will you go to

Philip F. O'Connor

Holman's and buy me a candy bar and I said nothing but took the money and went and brought it back and she said want to help me eat it and I didn't but I didn't know what to do so I nodded and she took me into the house and it was empty and she sat on the sofa just by the window and ate most of the candy bar herself, slowly, and said why are you looking at my legs, smiling at me and saying it, and then I spoke for the first time saying I don't know but I was looking at them and she held out the candy bar and nodded and then again until I came over and took a little bite and she said wasn't that good and I said yes very softly and she took my forefinger and said touch right here.

My brother and I used to lie under the weeping willow tree and rub ourselves against the grass until one day our mother saw us and called us inside and said what were you doing and we told her rubbing ourselves and she said that is a naughty trick and we must never do it again and if she caught us she would have to tell the priest. So we didn't do it again because we were afraid of the priest who had a voice like the thunder that came in from the ocean but we did talk about it, at night we talked about it, and I said what did it feel like to you and he said I don't know, what did it feel like to you, and I said it felt sweet and he said yes it felt sweet and we didn't question why we shouldn't do it but just talked about the sweetness, remembered it, and wanted to tell, at least I did, everyone about the sweetness, except the priest, but didn't.

There was a swimming pool at the far end of town and in the summer, his last summer, we started going there on our scooters even though it was far and our mother forbade us to swim and the girls wore bright swimming suits and lay on their backs and stomachs and we stood outside the fence and watched them, for hours we watched them with our eyes against the fence, and then we went home. It was going home from the swimming

142

pool that my brother got hit by a car and run over and killed.

"Now here," Sylvia said, "and now here," and I did it and did it wherever she said and the sweetness came over me and I squatted between her big legs while I did it and the room got hot and my clothes grew sticky and Sylvia leaned back against the curtain and wiggled and made soft sounds and finally she said, "That's enough. You better go home," and I did.

"Jesus came to save mankind which are serpents in the surrounding darkness and He has redeemed us from that darkness because He cast upon himself the flesh of man . . . ."

Sylvia went to Mass and wore a wide-brimmed white hat and sat up in front right next to the nun and when the priest's words began to frighten me I looked at her for she, her hat, never moved in the slightest as though she knew what he was going to say and lived by it and had nothing to fear, just looked upward saying yes with her eyes and that was all. I looked up too but was still afraid.

I was playing around the willow tree and my mother was hanging up the wash and Sylvia said over the back fence, "I'll make him lunch," and my mother said do you hear Sylvia and I said yes and she turned to Sylvia and said, "I think it's the best thing for him. He misses his brother." So I went.

She said I'm going to take a bath, do you want to watch, and I said I don't care but I did, I wanted to watch, and she filled the tub and took off her clothes and got in and the suds came up to her breasts and she told me to soap them, easy, and she put her head back on the rim and closed her eyes and said all over them, all over, and I did it all over until the sweetness came out of me, burst out of me, and flooded the room and the house and the neighborhood and the town. I fell forward into the tub and held her very tight my face between those enormous breasts. When it was over I cried.

She pushed me away and got up and dried very fast and said if you tell your mother I'll kill you and made me take off my clothes and put them in the oven until they were dry and hard and made me put them on and said, "Did you hear me what I said?" and I said yes and she said you're a little brat, I should have known, you acted crazy jumping in there on me, I should have known, don't come back. She was frightened more than angry. For once I seemed to understand her. But I didn't go back.

I went out by the willow tree one evening after supper to think about my brother because out there I remembered him happy as I didn't when I thought of him at other places. And then I heard Sylvia.

I crept over to the fence bordering her yard and listened but the sound was coming from someplace else so I went along the fence to the other fence, the one bordering the lot with the tall grass, and I heard her and she was saying, "You're too rough. You're too rough, David. Be easier." I listened and heard the grass swishing and her talking, chiding David, and after a while she stopped talking and the grass stopped swishing and I became frightened as though they were lying right in front of me, the two of them, staring back at me and waiting, waiting for something to happen to me, maybe doing something to me.

I crawled across our yard and slipped into our basement and sat in the blackness on the cold wet floor for a long time and feeling Sylvia and David in there with me, hanging from nails on the wall, one in front of me and one in back, leering at me with shiny teeth and panting, waiting, waiting for something, and then David growled and Sylvia came down off the wall and floated over to me, I was so sure of it I put my foot out to feel for her, she wasn't there, but still she was, pressing her great body down on me, crushing me into the concrete, saying "DON'T TELL! DON'T TELL! DON'T TELL!" Screaming it against my ears.

And I grew older and forgot or thought I forgot the sweetness but I was in a department store in the city and there were a lot of school girls around a counter where sweaters were on sale and my mother was someplace else in the store and I was waiting for her, I guess that was it. I got closer and closer to the girls and their skirts were short and when the girls moved about the skirts seemed alive with those bottoms dancing so softly beneath them and I had to do it and I did, I touched one of the bottoms so very gently but the girl spun about and then she screamed. The man came. My mother didn't believe him when he told her but all the way home from the city on the Greyhound she kept asking me, did I? did I? I didn't want to hurt her, she seemed so frightened. I said no.

My brother and I are rolling together in the tall grass of the lot through dream after dream and magically sinking into the earth when the big kitchen window opens and my mother shouts at us. And then we go flying invisibly, clinging together, up into the oak tree at the back of the lot when Sylvia and David lumber toward us making the ground shake. We hold each other and don't listen to the obscenities my mother roars from the big window and don't look as Sylvia and David kick and beat at each other on the grass until the oak tree trembles. We know there is something lovely in us holding, caressing, each other up here where no one can know us or touch us.

Powers Being Himself

Powers had just climbed onto a table in a Sausalito coffee house where the speech was advertised as free and poked his finger toward the ceiling, about to proclaim the joys of fatherhood and anarchy, when two cops came in and arrested him for indecent exposure. He had gone to the men's room and, thinking about what he was going to say on the table, turned from the urinal and forgot to zip up. When he cursed the cops in the courtroom later for scaring out of him the thoughts it had taken him half his lifetime to find, the judge ordered a psychiatric examination. He was found to be psychotic.

Every attempt at a door or window has been blocked; yet they keep giving him hope. They tell him he's not such a bad patient. With a little bending and a few nods he can be out in no time. Cooperate is the big word around here. Hang in there and swing with therapy. That sort of thing.

"The hell with you. I'm going out on my own terms or none."

"Really, Mr. Powers?"

"I got myself to protect."

"Indeed."

"You going to let my woman and the kid come and visit?"

"The rules, Mr. Powers. You understand."

147

"Up yours with the rules. Are you or aren't you?"

"We *can't,* Mr. Powers." They made *can't* sound like a pair of clapping hands.

He thought of breaking out. But he knew from his own experience and what the other patients said, everyone who tried got caught. He killed the thought, sure they had read it on his face and were adding months every time they saw it. He didn't bother to legalize his love, and that's why they won't let his woman and the baby come to visit. He tries to make them understand he's only being himself. Once he got up in group therapy after someone had pointed at him and said he looked the kind who would sell dope to childen. "I've never even taken pot, for Christ sake!" He left out that he'd tried but couldn't find any. The doctor in charge of therapy that morning told him that since a lot of people these days had tried pot it might be a sign of submerged paranoia that he hadn't. There was no winning. He fell into his chair and watched the doctor write something in his notebook. He quickly shut up. He thought of asking why some of the younger patients had been committed *just* for taking pot. He knew he wouldn't get an answer so he didn't ask.

The next question he asked was directed at his doctor: "What are the charges?"

Goosethorn only grinned and asked, "What exactly do you mean by charges, Mr. Powers?"

"You know what I mean. Read me the rap sheet. I want to know what I'm here for."

"This," said Goosethorn, showing a line of teeth like naked soldiers at attention, "is not a prison."

"It isn't, eh?" Powers had a little cap. Miranda, his woman, had given it to him. It was on his lap, for he carried it with him wherever he went. He snapped it onto his head, stood, smiled, and said, "I'll send the address where to mail my things." He headed for the door, turning as he opened it, giving Goosethorn a little wave with his fingers. "Thanks for your time." Meant it. Before he reached the double door at the end of the hall an elephant's burp sounded through the ward. The top half of the door snapped shut like a guillotine; had his arm been there it would have come off. "Je-suss!" In a moment two orderlies, off-duty wrestlers by the feel of them, had him by the shoulders and were dragging him back to Goosethorn's office. They dropped him into the patient's chair. Goosethorn was still behind the desk, fiddling with a pencil, still grinning. "Charges, Mr. Powers. I think you said something about charges."

"You god damn . . . lousy . . . ."

Goosethorn nodded encouragement.

". . . lousy . . . no good . . . ."

Perfect qualification, Goosethorn's face said.

". . . warden!"

Nice. Nice.

Powers ranted on for half an hour. Goosethorn wrote like a secretary trying to break the record for shorthand. Powers paused and watched him. He's already got his prize, Powers decided: me. He said no more.

That night he mailed Miranda the cap. "Hug it," he said in a little note snapped onto it in the button that held the bill to the top, "I'm going to be here a long time."

And has been.

Once Goosethorn asked him what *he* thought was wrong with himself but he said only, "Nothing. I forgot to zip up my pants. But nothing."

Then he got wise. In group therapy, listening to the patients who were close to release, he started putting it together. You had problems or you made them up. Then you made up ways of effectively dealing with them. You spoke with little surprises and insights and pauses, and you groaned now and then to show the pains of recognition, and you nodded silently to yourself at appropriate moments, as if coming across a chancre of illusion you hadn't been aware of; and, surrounding all else, had *A*

149

Problem, an enormous lump in which everything else was buried, an obsession (as the boys in the trade said), a thing you never stopped thinking or talking about. For the record at least you worked on it constantly. When you really had it figured out—for you'd never get rid of it—they began considering your release. Weeks. Months. It depended on how good you were at conning them, and maybe yourself.

Next to Powers at group therapy sat a redhead with a face like Babe Ruth. He was working at the Post Office when they captured him. Came in talking about the Communist pimps that had taken over the Post Office. "They're stealing Uncle Sam's mail and sending it to Russia. No use trying to do anything. No use. They're just about in control." He cried into the floor. Goosethorn, running group therapy that morning, tried to cross-examine him. What evidence? Oh shit, what evidence! He was weeping. He had seen it all: how they tampered with packages and letters! What evidence! He had reported his findings to the postal inspectors one day and the next day about twenty of the inspectors showed up and were peeking at the hippies working at the main branch, through cracks in the wall and holes in the floor and hidden windows behind the pigeonholes. "They arrested seven of them, for God's sake!" Under further questioning, however, it turned out that four of them had been charged with taking money and checks and the other three with eating things from the broken package bin: nuts and candy bars and things like that. "But how many for subversion?" someone asked. At which point the redhead grew very calm and quietly explained: "They could never charge them with the true crime. Everyone in the country uses the mails. Think of what a panic it would cause if the population found out what was really going on." The man apparently knew his history, pointing out all sorts of spy cases—the convictions weren't really for spying or sabotage but for perjury and crossing state lines and not paying taxes and so on. "Our leaders don't want to alarm us," he concluded, spreading his arms open and sending his dazzled eyes around the circle of attentive patients. "They have to protect us. They tell us nothing." Then, in a whisper: "But I observed and I *know*. Spies." After listening to the Babe, Powers was dizzy for three days. Not that Powers didn't appreciate the Commies at the Post Office story. That was a masterpiece. He himself could imagine nothing but his own true life. Of course it was possible that Babe was imagining nothing but *his* own true life. Seemed that way once he started to improve. He began to question himself out loud. "It could be they were only dupes. The Commies sold them drugs and got them to do the stealing." Still later: "Well, I can conceive of them doing the stealing only so they could eat and buy their dope. Still, it plays into the hands of the subversives." Pretty soon he was getting close enough to the biases of the times to be considered safe for out-patient care: he did a lot of groaning and moaning and squeezing of his temples. "I could have sworn they were Reds. I must have been in terrible shape. Wow. Nothing but filthy hippies. Imagine that." He almost had everyone convinced, including Powers, until the afternoon he was leaving for good. He asked Powers in the hallway if he knew whether or not cyanide was tasteless. Powers said he didn't and wondered why the Babe had asked. "Fhsshhhuuu." Babe looked at him from beneath thick red eyebrows as if any mongoloid ought to know: "Why d'ya think?" "Can't guess," Powers said. The Babe called him close and whispered, "I'm going to sprinkle it on the candy bars and nuts in the broken package bin, that's why." Powers recoiled. "Those Red devils don't have me fooled!" He grinned, knowing sure-as-hell no one would believe Powers if he squealed. Then he turned and slithered toward the double doors, both halves of which a smiling orderly was holding open for him.

After the redhead Powers began to hate. Doctors, nurses, even the other patients. Maybe one exception: Mr. Pollino. Pollino didn't go to group meetings very often. When he did go, he sat near the back and frowned at everyone. Powers started to ask questions, learned that Pollino had been here longer than anyone, rarely spoke to his doctor, exhibiting the worst symptom of all, silence. (Powers's symptom, worry, wasn't nearly as bad.) To Powers, Pollino was a mystery, and for that reason Powers started to like him. After his experience with the Babe, Powers began to sneak into Pollino's room at night. Pollino talked, admitted he had wine at the back of the closet. He offered some to Powers. Said he paid off the nurses.

"See what kind of a country it is?" Pollino said one night. "You can buy anybody."

"It's no surprise."

"Add it up. No one's safe. I bet my wife is selling herself right now."

"I believe it."

"You got a woman, eh?"

"Yep."

"She's probably a whore like my wife."

"Different."

"Bullshit."

"This one is different."

"You got some hope yet," Pollino said. "Me, I got none."

"Everybody's got hope."

"Not me. Do these look like hope?" He stuck out his wrists and turned them upsidedown. There were layers of scars on each.

"You got some or you wouldn't be sitting here drinking wine with me."

"I used to have hope but now I got no hope."

"Not me."

Powers took his word. He figured when you got to the

bottom and looked down and saw there was still someone underneath you had to like him. Powers, he liked
Pollino. One day Pollino was going to bleed out those
wrists before anyone could get to him in time to turn
them off. That worried Powers.

So did a lot of other things. Like him being an animal.
He was more of an animal than most patients. Take
with Mary Ginsburg, the pretty patient. Already he had
grabbed her down at the municipal swimming pool where
the social worker took them once in a while. Tried to
drag her into the empty men's dressing room and love
her. Mary got away and, thank goodness, kept her
mouth shut so no one found out. But here he was, a bud-
ding rapist on top of everything else. Better to be a trick-
ster like the Babe. Or even a suicide like Pollino. A
lot of other things are worrying him just now but to
hell with them. He feels like taking a walk in the Rose
Garden.

He doesn't give a diddly about the Rose Garden. It's
just the only place you can go when they let you out of
the building alone. You ask the nurse at the desk in the
hall and she says yes or no. This time she said no, it's
too close to supper time, but he waited until she left the
desk and went anyway. He slid over the bottom half of
the double door, ran down the stairs and went all the
way to the garden. He will pay for it later. They won't
let him go swimming or something. What the hell does
that matter?

He thinks of Pollino again. A few nights ago he told
Pollino he might not feel so lousy if he divorced his wife.

"Divorce my wife?" Pollino said. "What do I want
to do that for?"

"You said she cheats on you."

"Jesus Christ! Look at me! Wouldn't you cheat on
someone who looked like me?"

Pollino was truly an ugly man with his crooked eyes
and harelip and black teeth.

"It was just a thought," Powers said.

"On top of that I'm crazy, locked up in a crazy house. What do you expect of a woman?"

Maybe Pollino was right. Now he thinks maybe he should write to Miranda, that's his woman, and tell her not to wait for him. He is as ugly as Pollino, at least inside. He would write except for the baby. The baby was only as big as a cantaloupe last time he saw it. He held it up next to his cheek all the time and sang to it. Couldn't put it down. That was part of his sickness, they said. He loves Miranda too much anyway. Will want to be with her every minute when he gets out. He decides he's not going to write any letter. Not that kind anyway.

In the Rose Garden he puts his arms on the back of the bench and crosses his legs and watches through the big wire fence the people driving home from downtown San Francisco in their big expensive cars. He thinks of how comfortable they look. He thinks of miserable Pollino and how he is going to do himself in for good one of these days. Those comfortable people. Miserable Pollino. His thoughts go back and forth. He has lit a big cigar. He waves it at the passing cars and starts shouting. "You son-of-a-bitch! How come you're sitting there in that big rod when people have troubles? Huh?" The rich people look out of the car windows and wave at him, thinking, look at that nice friendly patient. How could they know?

If he sat around all day thinking of his worries, he'd never get out of his room. If you're all the time thinking about raping or killing people, you get so you can't move. When he isn't thinking of doing things to someone else, he's thinking of them doing things to him: not letting Miranda visit, not letting him go swimming, not telling him how many months or years it will be before they release him. Maybe one of these days he'll try to bust out after all. Go over that fence there. Sure, and then get caught and put in a room with a door that won't open. Worry, no matter what.

Recently, having given up on their therapy, he's begun to invent his own. He has found little ways for release. Like sometimes he sneaks down to the hospital waiting room and puts all the *New Yorkers* in a big ash tray and burns them. *New Yorkers* make him nervous, and he figures they make everyone else nervous too, or ought to. The ads especially. What kind of world was that in the ads? There's no such world. In ten years of looking at *New Yorker* ads he has yet to see a pair of wrinkled pants, and that's forgiving the ads where pants are for sale. He has always had wrinkled pants. He is sure the people in the Cadillacs even have wrinkled pants. What kind of a magazine is that? The stories too. He started reading the *New Yorker* in college. He wanted to be a writer and some teacher told him to read the stories in the *New Yorker*. He didn't finish college but he kept on reading the *New Yorker,* looking for something he never found. To hell with the *New Yorker*.

He wants to talk. He wants to ask the people in the cars, maybe about their tricks, the tricks that keep them outside the fence in the cars. Sometimes kids pass, on the way to the playground. He talks to them, but not with obscenities. The kids, high school, grade school, don't make fun of him or anyone else who might happen to be in the Rose Garden. Maybe they figure being in this place is like their own lives. Fathers are like doctors who figure they know everything. Mothers are like nurses enforcing the rules. And playground directors like social workers herding you here, herding you there, taking all the fun out of free time. Piss and shit on all of them. He wishes a kid would walk by with a basket- ball. He would talk to him about basketball. There are no kids.

He walks over to the fence. He breaks off a piece of

the vine that is growing on part of the fence. He throws
it over the fence at the next car that zooms by. It's a
black Buick, about three-years-old. The wood hits the
rear bumper. The car's brakes sound like an old woman's
shriek. The Buick hops up on the far curb and skids
along, two wheels on sidewalk, two on street, finally
coming to a stop. A stumpy man gets out, about forty,
eyes zigzagging all over the place. He walks around the
car, searching. He walks like he's sitting down, hunched,
big round bald head half-buried in his chest. He is
mumbling to himself.

"Nice day!" Powers yells.

The man is about fifty yards down the street. He looks
about, finally seeing Powers behind the fence. "Something hit my car," he calls back. "You see what hit
my car?"

"Yeah. Something from up there." Powers points to
the sky.

The man looks up.

"A little piece of something. I saw it coming down."

The man looks at his fender. He looks at the sky
again; it's very clear. He turns to Powers.

"It had a blue tail on it. A shiny blue tail."

Powers has seen a thousand like him. Vacant expression. Must be some kind of salesman. Spends his life
running from one customer to the next, depending on that
dumb expression of his to make each customer believe
there are no tricks up his sleeve. Never getting enough
to pay off the last car he bought. Badly fitting suit with
jacket buttons always open. Big loose wet lips that rarely
close. Car trunk probably loaded with cigars. Wife at
home stumbling over a frozen-food recipe. He comes
back from work and supper isn't ready: "Aw Christ,
Helen." That's all, but she throws the uncooked meal
on his suit.

He comes toward the fence where Powers waits. He
doesn't know what to make of the unshaved face or the

bathrobe. But he has to ask: "What kind of thing?"

"Like a sort of curved missile."

"A missile! You . . . you sure about that?" Probably worries all his life about things falling out of the sky and hitting him. Now something has. "A real missile?"

For some reason Powers likes him. He wiggles his finger. "Could you come a little closer?"

He does.

Powers looks warily to both sides, speaks softly. "I'm locked up here."

"Locked up?"

"A prisoner."

The man steps back. Looks up at the building. "Is this a prison?"

"Didn't you know that?"

"Nuh, no. I work out of L.A." He squints at Powers. "What kind of prison?"

"Political."

"Political?" he says loudly.

"Shut up, for Christ sake." Powers grips the fence with his fingers. "Come closer."

He hesitates, then comes up next to the fence.

Powers whispers. "Tell them to pick up Carlos in front of the Cuban Consulate."

"What?" He turns his head to the side so as to hear better.

"Carlos. He's one of them."

His face flashes back. "One of who?" he says, frightened.

"One of the others."

"Others?"

"I'm not one of them. For Christ sake, get that straight. I'm not one of them."

Suddenly he is nodding nervously. Getting it straight, Powers guesses. His eyes jump from the fence, to the building, to Powers. "What's this all about?"

"Life and death. If they don't pick up Carlos in front of the Cuban Consulate. He'll have a briefcase."

"Are you, are you sure you know what you're talking about?"

"Yes. And lower your voice. God damn it, don't you care?"

"I care, but."

"Then listen. Tell them Dave Harding gave you the word. Tell them they have to get Carlos or the waterfront is wiped out!"

"Wiped out!"

Powers takes a step back. "Got to go before the other prisoners see me. I'm counter espionage."

"Wait." His forehead is wrinkled. His face is flat against the fence.

"Carlos. It means everything." Powers backs up more.

"Wait! Wait!"

"You'll be doing your country a service, mister. It was me who hit your car. With my signal gun."

"Signal gun?"

"Made a little hole but don't worry. They'll pay for it."

"Who?"

"The ones you tell, damn it. Now hurry!"

The man sinks away from the fence. His hair is mussed. His jacket is all lopsided. He is stopped by a telephone pole against his back. His eyes search the universe. "What's this all about?"

Powers knows the orderlies will soon be around looking for him, bringing their fierce headlocks. As he hurries back to the bench, the salesman's words leaped after him:

"Who is it I tell? I forget? What's the name?"

"Anyone!" Powers shouts when he gets to the bench. "Tell anyone! The whole country knows what's happening. Everyone, apparently, except you."

The man is in the middle of the street. He checks Powers, the building, his car. He turns this way, then that, and finally runs for the car, maybe it's all he's got to run for.

Powers sits down. He wants to think about the salesman, remember what happened, enjoy it, later tell Pollino. He is alone for about thirty seconds. Here come a
couple of orderlies.

"Go away!" he shouts.

"Time for supper," one of the orderlies says.

"I'm having a daydream," he says. "Let me have it.
It may be important. Goosethorn may want to hear about
it. So go away."

They are almost upon him when a scream, a long
piercing scream, leaps down at them from the top floor
of the building. He recognizes the voice. It's Pollino.
"Run!" he says to them, "he's killing himself again!"

They run.

Before they reach the building entrance he calls to
them. "At the back of the closet! Wine bottles! He
probably cut his wrists with a broken bottle! Take the
bottles away!"

They vanish into the building.

Pretty soon he slumps forward on the bench, angry at
himself for having called to them about the wine bottles.
Suddenly angry. If Pollino wants to kill himself, that's
his business. He feels like a traitor. He puts his head
between his legs. He says, "Shit." He means himself.

Later he finds enough strength to drag himself into
the building and up the stairs. One floor, two floors.
When he gets to the third floor, he thinks of Miranda
and the baby. He cries. For no god damn good reason
he cries. Very weak, he holds onto the banister and
puts his head down and cries. Nurses pass, interns pass,
visitors pass. No one seems to know what he's doing.
Maybe he's throwing up. What do they know?

When he stops crying he's mad, blind mad, but he
knows he can't tear down the banister or slug someone
because then he'll never ever get out and see Miranda
and the kid, not that his chances are good as it stands.
So he goes back downstairs. Having thought of some-

thing, he holds onto the banister and pulls himself down the stairs.

In the waiting room there is an old man who looks like he's been dead for twenty years, a visitor, not even a patient. He's sitting in a corner. Powers picks up all the *New Yorkers* and piles them in a big ash tray and says, "Mister, you got a match?" The old man bends his skinny arm and reaches into his coat pocket, bringing out one of those big wooden matches and handing it, puzzled, to Powers. "Will you lend me your foot?" Powers says. "Eh?" The old man bends forward. Powers kneels down, impatient, raises the man's foot, strikes the match—he himself is wearing slippers with frictionless bottoms—and sets the *New Yorkers* going. Powers thinks the old man will say something, but the old man doesn't, just sits there gazing as the *New Yorkers* go into flames about two feet high, and then into cinders which float about the room, and then into smoke which begins to coat the ceiling; sits there and doesn't change the expression on his face. Someone is burning papers in an ash tray for some reason, that's all.

On the way upstairs Powers thinks, what a funny world.

He goes to Pollino's door and opens it.

Pollino is not dead. He's cursing. "They took my wine away," he says. "I stubbed my toe on the bed and yelled and they came and took my wine away." He looks at Powers. "What do you think of that? What the Christ do you think of that?"

"Criminal!"

"Some lousy son-of-a-bitch must of squealed."

"The dog!"

"But I got another bottle under the radiator. Go get it."

Powers does, and brings it back to Pollino's bed and opens it and they drink, careless of passing attendants.

Funny, my ass, Powers thinks as he takes a swallow.

Gerald's Song

My stocks have descended, my stocks are in pottery and my stocks have descended. The soldiers destroy all the pottery where they are fighting, my stocks are in the company which imports that pottery, other things are up but my stocks are down. Down because of the war in that country where there is pottery.

Once I said the boys are giving up their lives so I should not complain. I did not start the war, I do not like the war, I put my money in pottery not bullets, but I should not complain. The fighting boys have a right to complain but I should not complain. It didn't work.

I have my mother to think of. I live with her, I buy her things, she is tiny and pale and moves with a creak. She worries that I will have nothing when she dies. She says, *how is the pottery,* I say *down,* she bends and she whistles and she says, *O Gerald.*

The pottery looked good, the pottery had a future, the pottery was a sure thing. I put all of my money, the money my father left me, in the pottery. The pottery has gone down to a dollar, has nearly vanished.

O Gerald.
O Mother.

I have wanted to do something, I have wanted to write to the stock exchange, I have wanted to write to the newspaper, I have wanted to write to the President. It

161

Philip F. O'Connor

is not good, this war, it is not good for any of us, but what can I do, what can I say, I can only fret and what does that change.

O Mother.

O Gerald.

People can love each other, it was in the hope of people loving each other that I picked pottery, pottery could let us know about other people, civilization is to be found in pottery, I was hopeful when I put my money into it, I thought of poor families eating better because of the market for their pottery. I did not invest solely to make a profit. He who does that would be sinful.

O Gerald.

O Mother.

We look in the shops on Sunday, my mother and I, we look in the windows and pick out things for each other. My mother does not walk well, I stop with her for tea, she says, *Gerald, you will look divine in that cravat.* O, my heart is heavy. O, my soul is heavy. Soon there will be no more cravats. *It's the war, Mother, I have put everything in pottery and now there is the war.*

The war the war.

O Mother.

The war is taking everything away.

I did not want to be a soldier, I could never have been a soldier. Her cousin helped us, he was on the draft board, it was not unfair, she was getting old, I could not go to the Army with my mother getting old, I did not go. I stayed home and we played chess. She said, *what are you going to do with your father's money.* I said, *put it in pottery.* She said, *are you sure that's wise.* I said, *pottery can't lose.*

O the war the war. What am I to do?

The President said we have to be there, I believed him, then the Secretary of State said we have to stay there, and I believed him, then our congressman said we have to bring this to a successful conclusion or we can't show

162

our faces anywhere in the world, and I believed him. I believed them all. But the pottery is down and my mother is getting older.

Gerald, you must do something.

What can I do?

You must do something. I will worry myself sick if you don't.

What can I do?

Don't let me down now.

What can I do?

O Gerald.

O Mother.

She threw her teacup. It struck me on the forehead. *Do something, you stupid boy,* she said, *do something.*

I called our congressman and wired the Secretary of State and wrote a letter to the President. They all told me in one way or another that the war can't be stopped. I said to her, *they can't stop it.* I said, *once in it's hard to get out. I know that from the pottery.*

You are as stupid as the government, she said.

No one could have predicted.

As stupid as the government.

I'm sorry, Mother.

What did you want with pottery anyway?

I wanted to help the people in other countries.

Let the sons-of-bitches help themselves.

I'm sorry, Mother.

In your father's day we let them help themselves. It was better.

Yes, Mother.

O Gerald, why can't they stop the stupid war?

I wish they would.

We'll be poor if they don't stop the war.

Yes, Mother.

I went to my broker. I said, *what can I do?*

He said, *you shouldn't have invested in pottery.*

Philip F. O'Connor

I said, *but you told me to.*

He said, *brokers make mistakes too. We are only human.*

I said, *do you have money in pottery?*

He said, *my money is in bullets. I was lucky.*

I said, *what can I do?*

He said, *wait and hope. When the pottery goes up we'll sell and put the money in bullets.*

The pottery didn't go up.

My mother kicked the coffee table. She said, *I have always lived well. I don't intend to live any other way now. I am old. My arthritis is acting up. How could you do this to me, Gerald?*

I'm sorry, Mother.

She spit at me. She wiggled her arms in the air. *How could anyone be so stupid?* She cursed and tried to get up. I think she was going to attack me. She fell back. She nearly fell to the floor.

Take it easy, Mother.

Who can take it easy on the way to the poorhouse?

O Mother.

I am used to comfort, Gerald, and you are taking it from me.

O Mother.

O Gerald.

They didn't stop the war, my pottery is down to thirty cents, I have taken to not coming straight home after my work at the library, I have taken to stopping for a drink, I have another drink and then another and then I worry that my mother has fallen off her chair and I go home. She is always awake, sitting rigid, staring down my shirt front, saying *Gerald, you were always a dope.*

I can't bear the looks she gives me, that's why I drink, I didn't try to lose my money, I didn't ask for the war, it is too late to get my money out now, I feel I am going down, we are all going down, I don't want to go down,

164

this is my life and I want to live it, I don't understand the war, politics bore me, speeches bore me, I want more interesting things, I like books, I read about pottery when it's not busy in the reference room, I used to enjoy reading about pottery, now it makes me sick, but it is my interest, I read about it, pottery is made all over the world, there are different kinds of pottery for different countries, pottery is one of the oldest things made, Mexican pottery is very pretty, my mother is old and dying, I didn't start this war, it was a happy country before the war, people could pursue their interests, pottery was mine, it still is, I don't enjoy it as much as I used to, the war makes it less interesting, the war makes my mother irritable, the war is taking my money away, we have a hard time getting page boys at the library, they are all going into the army, why must they go, why must we fight, who knows why we are fighting, who knows what's important about that little country, what has happened that we don't know, what has happened that the congressman and the senator and the President can't help us, why is there war, who are those people we are fighting, what do they want with us, I would have gone on investing in their pottery, they could have made lots of money selling their pottery in this country, did they sell it in another country, is that why we are fighting them.

There is a war and I don't understand it, there is a war and I don't understand it, there is a war and I don't understand it.

O Mother.

O Gerald.

Blather

She a mother and he her son. Living under the same roof they were for thirty-six years, she waiting on him hand and foot, getting the few pennies she could by housekeeping at the local rectory and he not giving a nod of thanks, big stump of a thing devouring and cursing and sleeping half his life away, never lifting a hand to help:

"Michael, when are you going out and find yourself a job?"

"Never."

So she worked herself weary, poor woman, while he sat at home and read books. Scandalous books they were, filled with coarse women, not that he'd ever given a thought to a proper girl, to say nothing of marriage.

"Michael, you'll be the death of me."

"Something will, that's sure."

"What is it you find in those books anyway?"

"A world I never knew."

She went to the pastor.

"God knows, Father, I've done my level best."

"You have *that*," he said with a shake of his shaggy Galway head.

"If there was only a little hope."

"Ah, but there isn't, Alice." Hadn't he suffered

through countless suppers listening to her stories about the cur. "If there was even a ray of hope, you can be sure I'd have got in touch with O'Brien, the contractor, or Bellini, the sanitation man, and found him an honest job."

"He wouldn't last a day, Father."

"Don't I know it?"

"Oh, Father, what's there to do?"

"I wouldn't like to say."

"I'm desp'rit, Father," she said with a sob.

He sucked on his black pipe until it popped and said, "Bring me my cup of tea."

She went to the kitchen and got it and brought it back and wiped the crumbs from his place and put it down.

"Sit down across there," he said, pointing to the chair on the other side of the table.

She went around with a sigh and settled into the chair, letting her hands fall into the valley of her apron.

He took a sip of tea and then lifted his pipe and spoke into the bowl as if it were a microphone that put him in touch with Heaven. "Have the poor creature sent to the State House," he said.

"Oh, Father."

"If there was another way, you can be sure I'd tell it to you."

"I suppose," she said with a little gasp. "I suppose."

She did the dishes and helped him count the collection and then turned down his bed. When he saw her to the door he gave her hand a little squeeze. "Faith, woman," he said. "Faith."

When she arrived home, she found Michael with his head buried in one of his books.

"I'm going to have you put away," she told him.

"You do what you want," he said, and he turned a page without even lifting his head. His eyes went down the page and his tongue went round and round. "Chaazusss, there's a lady in here turns me upsidedown!"

He was far gone. The priest was right. When Michael was asleep she made her call.

They came and quietly took him out of bed.

"Still and all," she told Father the next day, "it's not going to be easy without him."

"But all for the best," he said with a certainty that soothed her nicely.

The house seemed dark and empty without him and every time she'd pull a book out from under a bed or chair and see the pages all turned down and the red crayon circles and the white all blackened where his fingers had squeezed the pages her thoughts went after him and she wept. To cheat her loneliness she spent more time at the rectory.

"When do you think they'll let him out, Father?"

"Ah sure," he said, flicking the stem of his pipe toward the ceiling, "some of those cures take years."

"I don't know how I'll put up with the waiting."

"You're free of him now." He snapped the pipe stem toward her. "Be grateful."

"I suppose I should."

"Indeed you should." He held out his cup. "Warm this up a bit."

She made fruit cake and sent it to Michael and got warm socks for his birthday and at the bottom of the Easter card she told him to ask the officials if she could be allowed to take a bus up some Sunday evening for a visit.

All he did was return a list of books he told her she could get in the bookstore at the back of the alley near the cathedral, the one he used to visit when she stopped for a rosary on their trips to the city. If she happened to be going that way.

She wouldn't, of course, be found dead purchasing one of those books of his, though as the days passed and the sound of his voice faded from her memory she was nearly

Philip F. O'Connor

tempted. "I don't know how I'll put up with the waiting," she said to herself more than once in the months that followed. She did little extra jobs at the rectory to fill in the time.

"It's not easy, Father."

"No one ever said it would be."

One lonely night when she was nearly asleep there came a rapping on her window and she looked up to see what appeared to be the black hulk of a gorilla in the pear tree by her room.

"God all mighty!"

"Mother, why did you lock the door?"

"Michael!"

"Will you stop shouting and open this god damn window! The branch is about to give out!"

In the moonlight she could see his face flatten grotesquely against the pane. "God help us," she whispered. The valves of her heart closed a bit and she sat up, catching her breath.

"Are you deaf or what?" he shouted.

She squinted and saw that he'd gone down a foot or two. She sent her feet to the floor in search of her slippers. "Just a minute now," she said, "just a minute." She pushed and kicked, panted and wheezed, finally got the heaviness of herself off the bed.

"What the hell are you doing now?"

"Looking for my other slipper." She went to her knees to reach under the bed saying, "Be patient, you ungrateful pup, waking me up with a fright like . . . ."

There was a loud crack and a terrible roar.

She turned her head. "Michael!" she shouted.

He'd vanished into the night.

She found him several minutes later tangled in the clothesline he'd tied to the pear tree for her instead of taking the trouble to put a pole in the ground.

"I'm here, Michael. I'm here," she said from the basement door.

170

He turned on her with a stream of curses that went on until she had him untied. "It's your own fault," she told him. "Your own fault."

He'd calmed down a little by the time she'd got him to the kitchen table.

"What on earth brought you back at an hour like this?"

"I ran off. Where's my books?"

"I didn't get them."

"Just like you."

She made warm milk, then helped him to his room, saying, "Michael, I'll never make sense of you."

"You weren't meant to."

The next morning she cooked him a big breakfast and said several prayers of thanks that he'd come back safe and sound. She knew it was wrong he'd run off but not until nearly noon did she find the strength to tell him he'd have to go back.

"I won't go back."

"Oh, you must, Michael."

"I won't."

"You'll have to, Michael. Those are the rules."

He had a way of charming her. She could see it coming now with the smile he gave her. Rare that he used it but when he did: "Give us a little whiskey, Mither, for old times sake. We'll discuss it."

"Go on with you now."

"You and I, Mammy. A bit of a snort."

"Stop the Irish talk. You know what it does to me."

"I'll keep it up. I'm as Irish as you."

"You're not. You were born in America."

"So was Eamon de Valera. Give us a drink."

She knew what was right and what was not. "There'll be no drink. They haven't cured you at all."

"I was ready. If you'd mailed me me books I'd have stayed a little longer, but I was ready all the same."

"Oh, Michael."

"O, Mither, me love." He was in best form. "The whiskey."

"Get it yourself, you cur."

He did. He poured them each a drink. "Did I tell you what they did to me?"

"You've told me next to nothing."

"They beat me with a whip and made me denounce the Pope."

"Are you trying to age your poor mother more than she's aged already?"

"It's the truth. And the reason you couldn't visit is because they blamed you for all my troubles."

"I don't believe you."

"They said what sort of pleasure do you get out of those books and I told them great pleasure and they said why did I think that was and I told them the ladies were well presented and they said did I not think it strange that I found my only ladies in books and I said no and they said what does your mother think of the books and I said she doesn't like them and they said ah ha!"

"What did that mean?"

"They said it was you who put me onto the books in the first place."

"I never did!"

"They said you didn't give me nearly the love I deserved, not since I was born, and I turned to those ladies in your place."

"Jesus, Mary and Joseph!"

"Let me finish. They said what do you think of your mother. I said she cooks a good potato. They said what do potatoes mean to you. I said life. They said would I mind explaining that. I said my ancestors had the good sense to bury a lot of them in the ground before the famine or else I wouldn't be here. Therefore life."

"Did you really say that?"

"I did. They kept on about you and the potatoes, going once in a while to the apples and peaches on the ladies I admired in my books. I told them a string of

172

tales as long as your rosary and they were very interested."

"What kind of tales?"

"Of banshees and leprechauns."

"Did you?"

"I did."

"And what did they think of them?"

"They said the tales weren't important in themselves.
All make-believe. They said I ought to think about what
they meant to me. They said unless I did that I'd never
be free."

"What's there to figure out, sure? They're just stories."

"Not in that place they're not. So I figured them out
the way they wanted. Pretending, you understand. I
said the little leps represented me and my childlike
innocence and the awful screeching banshees represented
you and the terror you struck in me that prevented me
from growing up the same as others."

"Me!"

"They'd have it no other way. They said I was making
it a bit simple but had it right in the main. They said
you see what she's done to you, don't you? I had no
choice. I said I did."

"The devils!"

"The very. The next day I cursed you to the sky and
every time they mentioned your name. It was the only
way. I said the bitch kept me under her apron all my life
or I wouldn't have sunk the fingers of my eyes into the
pages of those books . . . ."

"That's a lie!"

"Of course it is. But it got 'em to let me walk in the
Rose Garden. They wouldn't have let me walk if I
hadn't damned your soul."

"The bastards."

"The very. So yesterday I jumped the wall."

She sat down and looked at her hands. "Wait 'til I
tell Father."

"Don't. He's with them."

"I think you're right," she said, looking up. "But what in God's name do I do?"

"No need for a quick decision. Find a drop of the sweet nectar and pour us both a glass. They say St. Jerome used to have a couple every morning before he went out to face the heathens."

"Who says?"

"All that write books about him. Drink up now. It'll clear the demons out of your brain."

"It's other demons I'm worried about now. Did they really say all those things, Michael?"

"Indeed they did."

She tried to stand, but the weight of the conversation had taken its toll—"I'm worn to a frizzle."—and sent her back to her chair. "You can't return."

"I won't."

"I've kept you the first thirty-six years," she said with a sigh, "and I'll keep you the next thirty-six."

"There's no other way."

Mastodon's Box

I have locked myself in this room and won't go out. I have been here seven days by my calculations, which aren't very good. People have come to this door. Voices have said, "We will get you out." I have said, "Go away. I will shoot you if you don't go away." I have said that even though I don't have a gun or anything else that will shoot through a door.

Ring ring.

The phone.

Ring ring.

That would be she again, wanting me home.

Ring ring.

I ignore it.

Ring ring.

It stops.

On my bookshelf there are a hundred-and-thirteen books. The predominant book cover color is green but red comes in second. If you take the dust jackets off the books that have them, which seems a scientific thing to do, the book covers in their naked state come out with red slightly ahead. I have for my own stupid amusement deduced that book jacket designers have different tastes than book cover designers, and would honest-to-god like to report this in, say, *Designer's Journal,* for it is one of the few original discoveries I have ever made, as open as it might be to question.

As for what is between the covers of those books, who can say? As for what is between the covers of those books, maybe too much has already been said. As for what is between the covers of those books, I can tell you this much and no more: I have absolutely nothing to say.

Though I am not sure why I am in this room, I think it may have something to do with books. If I go on talking about books I may come to the precise and demonstrable reason why I am in this room, and, though I am unbelievably unhappy in this room, the last thing I want to do is figure out why I am here.

We were talking the night before I came into this room, my wife and I. It was a screwy conversation, as most of ours have been:

"Why can't you stay home and read a book?"

"I want to go to my room and do my work."

"You never stay home. You don't read anymore. You don't put the children to bed. The children miss you putting them to bed."

"I will do those things if you want me to but I don't myself want to."

"You do what you want."

"That's what I was planning to do but then you spoke."

"I spoke because I care."

"You spoke and took the joy out of me going to my room and doing my work."

"Your work, your work. What is your work? What is putting things on paper? How can that be work? What good comes of putting things on paper?"

"It seems important to me."

"Seems important, seems important. What is more important than your family?"

"My work. Sometimes my work."

"Your work. Hah."

176

"Yes. My work."

"What have I married? A man who works and puts his work in a drawer. A man whose work is nothing. A man whose work, which is nothing, puts his nothing-work before his wife and children."

"It seems important."

"Stop saying that. Don't *we* seem important?"

"Yes, you too."

"A rotten lie."

"I am not going to work."

"Go. You want to go. So go."

"It is now impossible for me to go to work."

"You are going. I will not have you sitting around here looking at me as though I prevented you from doing something."

"I can't go to work now."

"Go."

"I'm going, but I'm not going to work."

"Where are you going? To a bar, I suppose."

"I never go to bars."

"Mastodon!"

Slam!

In the metal drawer now open a few inches from my belly, there lies a mass of white sheets of paper which over the days/months/years have come to record the projections, geometric, of the turnings of my soul. Black on white, the offspring of the reason for my presence at this institution: I am its residential artist. Few of the drawings are complete. They interest me little, after the fact. I make no sense of them. The hand that draws them, however, has kept me, and her, and the children, in food and respectability, and for that I should be grateful. Yes, am grateful.

Once I fancied it floating down the main hall, my hand, and stopping in the doorway of the chairman of my department, there hovering, thumb and forefinger moving like the mouth of a rabbit one might project on a wall for a child, saying, "This is all of him you employ. Let the rest of him remain at peace. No more classes. No more memos or directives. No more service on committees for the assassination of unpalatable instructors, no matter how unpalatable. No more of your games. Load his office with paper and pen and black ink, then avast out of there."

My mother, a great Irish tub of butter, once said, why do you draw.

I said I don't know mother.

She said other boys have paper routes and all that is is scribbling.

I said my hands need work.

She said you could throw papers on porches and bring your poor mother a few pennies.

I said I feel vomity when I think of work.

She said you're seventeen going on eighteen and can't sit around drawing all your life.

I said I'm thinking of going to an art college and getting myself a degree.

She said when is that.

I said when it becomes too painful for me to sit and listen to you harping.

How long will it take you to get a degree or whatever it is?

As long as it takes me to draw as many as they require you to draw before they let you out I guess.

Go on to school then.

I will.

God knows its better than you sitting on your arse around here day and night.

My drawings have been shown three times. Four have been sold. Have made $112. Present position at institution resulted not from drawings or reputation conjured therefrom, but from Master of Fine Arts I had engraved, then printed, after leaving art school. Exodus followed tantrum by art instructor, who, while looking at my work, shouted, "You are going nowhere and never will!" Made up name of an art school, Barnaby Institute, and gave myself a *cum laude;* it looked real.

Have just drawn man, lines, holding spool, which extends to side of page. That is, thread, string or rope, extension of spool, itself lines, reaches out to side from man sitting holding spool or as if holding spool.

Turn it this way.

Turn it that.

Ring ring.

The phone again.

I answer quickly: "What, what, what?"

She: "Come out, Mastodon. The children want you to take them to the circus."

"No."

"It has been five days, Mastodon."

"I would not have guessed."

"They want me to send for a doctor. O, Mastodon, why do you . . . ."

Receiver reached cradle before last syllable uttered.

The books on the shelves on the wall behind me. Blake, Nietzsche, Thompson, Menson, Verhredule, Hjkinhygtrfdsssssss.

The drawing on the desk before me.

The walls. The window. The floor. The door.

He is winding in the spool. Or winding out the spool. He is a single line, entirely a single line making unbroken entry into spool, which is also part of single line extending further to sort of thread/string/rope, which goes dipping toward corner of page and is extension of same line, that is line composing spool and also man holding spool.

The chairman said, "The students complain that you disparage books on art, that you only draw lines on the blackboard, that you speak only in answers to questions."

"If I run out of blackboard space I use a pad, if I have one with me."

"Then, they claim, you have them draw what you call 'self-generating' lines."

"It is true."

"Any sort of lines they want."

"Always."

"Is that education, Mr. McGuire?"

"I don't know."

"You see what I'm driving at, don't you, Mr. McGuire?"

"No."

"Direction, Mr. McGuire. Purpose."

"I too seek . . . ."

"What faculties are you developing by having them draw lines in such a fashion?"

"I'm not sure."

"You called one of your drawings 'The French Dream.' Why is that?"

"It reminded me of a . . . a . . . ."

"You see, Mr. McGuire. You see why I've called you here."

"I don't."

"Something will have to change."

Her brother, George, a bartender, saw a luminescent green vehicle descend from sky and alight on road one evening as he was returning from work. Slowed down for closer look but vehicle rose out of sight. Occurrence reported simultaneously by brother-in-law, a farmer who'd gone to barn to silence a whimpering cow, and a *Mohawk Airlines* pilot flying to Ottawa. George has long not spoken to me but I asked my wife to tell him I believe Magellan might have seen such a vehicle. She refused.

Later she said, "Mastodon?"

"What?"

"George agrees. You should submit yourself to a doctor."

"As the green vehicle submitted itself to him, I suppose."

"Your're badly in need of help, Mastodon."

"If I had been with him I might not have seen the green vehicle, though it had been there; and yet I might have."

"Are you listening to me at all?"

Spool may in fact not be a spool but a wheel of sorts. Viewed from the side, it is difficult to tell. Though if I held paper up to light and looked from back I would be seeing it from other side. Yes, but that side would still be the first and only side; profitless effort therefore. Wheel or maybe reel. The other line perhaps a cable. Wheel and cable. Or reel and fishing line. If so, where is pole? Part of fishing line might be looked on as pole.

Her legs surrounded her buttons. Last night? I don't remember.

I, beside her, prostrate.

On the screen an early Hitchcock movie, English of the Thirties: on a train, stranded somewhere in the Alps, there hides a murderer.

I said, "Marcy?"

She said, "Quiet, Mastodon."

I said, "There is something in this movie I would like to speak to you about."

She said, "Twenty-seven, twenty-eight, twenty-nine, thirty."

The train whistled up a slope. My thoughts trailed it, then fled. I remembered having seen Alfred pictured in a Sunday rotogravure feature. He was standing at the butt of a movie camera. He was looking in the same direction as the movie camera, into the camera that was taking his picture. His mouth was open. He was, or seemed to be, gasping. I saw there the mouth of a man who either had just been killed or who was just about to kill: wordless, intense, and (if I was right) prepared to laugh off whatever the disaster. On the floor I made something of a connection and chose to share it:

"To begin with, Marcy . . . ."

"Forty-*five*, forty-six, forty-seven . . . ."

Philip F. O'Connor

"About the movie, Marcy. I see . . . ."

". . . forty-eight, forty-nine, fifty."

She put the reds across from the greens and the whites in near her crotch, leaving the odd ones on the periphery. I sat partly up, thinking to help her count, but I recalled that that morning she had said my breath was a horror— "Please don't come close to me!"—and, certain that the day's ham salad, Bulgarian salami and cocktail onions could only have turned horror to abomination, I went back, fully extended, to the floor, saying, "Though old and gray like my mother before her passing, Marcy, this movie consumes me in a way that our conversation, yours and mine, might have had we met, aged seventeen, on a seashore, having been blown there by a sensual blue and carefree wind in the middle of, oh, September."

"Did you kiss the children tonight?"

"No. I forgot."

They were all, in the train, rather ordinary Alfreds, all but one. In the murderer, I concluded, Alfred found himself, the way to hold the crowd and be the crowd and have the crowd, the Alfreds in the crowd, the boredom that was the crowd. The murderer, in short, was Alfred, who, when discovered, ended the movie about himself, fearing, I presumed, permanent identification. Further, he had the good sense to put two funny men on the train. They drank and made jokes with the other passengers, jokes I have now forgotten as I forget all jokes I hear, and the two of them eventually, as I recall, stumbled upon the killer. If bored with the search for Alfred, the audience had, at least, laughter.

"Marcy," I said, "I really wish you'd watch this movie. There's a lot more to it than just story. What's behind it, what I think is behind this movie, is fascinating. It has to do with art."

"Just a minute. I've lost one."

"The movie, Marcy."

"Oh, Mastodon, is life for you nothing but small amusements?"

182

Could put a sort of dot in middle to represent where pole end and fishing line be . . . .

Where is pen?

Can't find pen.

Have misplaced pen.

Unless someone entered and: "Hello?"

No one.

I think I detect the knob turning. "Are you there and did you take my pen?" Is the knob turning? Maybe the knob is not turning.

Up. Over. See.

No. The knob is not turning.

Back and down.

Ring ring.

Explode!

Ring ring.

Disintegrate!

Ring ring.

I pick it up: "What?"

"A humiliation. The neighbors are talking about a petition. My brother says this is grounds for annulment. Mother wants me to fly to Des Moines. You no longer have a job. Dr. Eppiletti says George was right. And . . . ."

Rip rip.

The phone was connected to the wall, is not now connected to the wall.

It was after the movie, I think, that I began to plan exit toward this room. I stood, directed myself into the hallway, heard a bear growl, turned in alarm though the bear was only my stomach, turned again, started for the kitchen, stopped, saw the telephone on the telephone stand, picked it up and threw it crashing to the floor.

"What a childish way to get attention!"

"My mother was born in Ireland," I said, for that's what happened to lie on the surface of my tongue.

"What are you talking about?"

"Suppose I found her, though dead, creeping about this house."

"Oh, Mastodon."

"If I did, Marcy, I would say, 'What do you think of my work, Mother?' She would say, 'Is that the sort of thing you've been wasting your years at?' I would say, 'Go in that room over there and meet my wife, who fell from the sky after your death, and tell me what you think of her.' She would go in there with you. She would not come out. I would wait but she would not come out. The two of you would chat like a pair of Homer's sirens on a lunch break. In about an hour she would call to me, saying, 'Mastodon, you don't appreciate what a *love*-ly partner-in-life you have. You have ignored and ill-treated her. You are no better than you were as a boy. I know just how she feels, Mastodon. Just.' You, Marcy, would then say, 'Your mother understands me, Mastodon, which you never have.' You would try to go on, but before you could I would interrupt. I would say, 'Shut your flappin' mouths, both of you. I understand your demands, but not your aims and principles.'"

Buttons clenched. "Won't you go up and see the people at the state hospital in Ogdensburg, Mastodon? A visit costs nothing."

"I should, Marcy. Things being what they are, I should."

"Of course you should."

"But I won't, preferring as I do to flee to a closet of my own making, to await the reappearance of my mother, or a mad art collector, or the Grand Entrepreneur himself. I've let myself have an outburst and it's come, as usual, to nothing. My own fault."

"Well, it's certainly not mine or the children's."

"That's certain."

"Mastodon, why did you marry me?" With that she went to bed, it being a question to which she did not expect, and would not have gotten, an answer.

The movie ended. I thought I should have pulled more out of it than I had. I got up. I followed her scent up the stairs. When I got into bed she rolled over and plunged her toenails into my leg. Her toenails are hard as wood. I rolled away. She said, "Mastodon, you take up so much room." I took one blanket and rolled down onto the floor.

I was nearly asleep when I felt something in my blanket. I reached down and pulled it out. The room was dark and I couldn't see it but I could feel it. A button, a very small button which was, I think, the reinforcing button from inside the flap just above the zipper on one of my pants. I reached up and put it very carefully on the bedside stand where she would see it.

In the morning I came to this room and remained.

Fishing pole impossible if, even if, dot added to represent where pole breaks and line begins, for pole/rod/ whatever and thread/string/rope/cable/whatever blend perfectly together and it is even hard to tell where spool/ wheel/reel begins or is it ends. Unless.

"Mastodon!"

She outside now. Voice seems to be climbing the building.

"Speak to me! Hurry! It's cold!"

Unless that line going out could be viewed as something else.

"All morning and all afternoon the children have been calling for you."

But what something else?

"Calling for you! Did you hear that, Mastodon?"

Whop! Snowball just hit my window.

"Did you hear?"

Have never much liked to fish anyway.

"I know you're there! Your light is on!"

Won't add another line. Cheating. Like cheating.

"Answer me, you crazy man! Answer me!"

Is that figure, in fact, a man at all? Looks now like a

Philip F. O'Connor

bull. Bull holding fishing pole. No, bull crouched. Not holding fishing pole. Holding what?

"Mastodon!"

His tail? No. That would be in back.

Whop!

He's holding his . . . holding his . . . o, my goodness . . . holding his . . . and is a bull pissing . . . .

"You heartless dog!"

A dog, or a bull, or a bear, pissing. A bear. The bear is holding its. No. It is not a bear, or a bull or a man.

I don't know what it is.

186